RAVES FOR
JAMES PATTERSON
AND HIS NOVELS
ALONG CAME A SPIDER

"A first-rate thriller—fasten your seat belts and keep the lights on."
—**Sidney Sheldon**

"As engrossing as it is graphic, *Along Came a Spider* is an incredibly suspenseful read with a one-of-a-kind villain who is as terrifying as he is intriguing. Has to be one of the best thrillers of the year."
—**Clive Cussler**

"What a large charge it is to come upon such a good writer so unexpectedly."
—**Richard Condon**

"All at once comes *Along Came a Spider,* with terror and suspense that grabs the reader and won't let go. Just try running away from this one."
—**Ed McBain**

more . . .

BLACK MARKET

"A taut thriller that rivals the best of Ludlum and Follett."
—*Chattanooga Times*

"A gripper!"
—**United Press International**

"A tough, twisting tale that will keep even the bulls and bears reading past the opening bell."
—*New York Daily News*

"You cannot put it down ... tense, gripping ... pays off in gilt-coated, hard-edged entertainment."
—*Atlanta Journal & Constitution*

"A gripping, fast-moving yarn that will keep the reader turning pages."
—*Houston Post*

SEASON OF THE MACHETE

The novels of James Patterson
FEATURING ALEX CROSS

Double Cross

Cross

Mary, Mary

London Bridges

The Big Bad Wolf

Four Blind Mice

Violets Are Blue

Roses Are Red

Pop Goes the Weasel

Cat & Mouse

Jack & Jill

Kiss the Girls

Along Came a Spider

THE WOMEN'S MURDER CLUB

The 6th Target (and Maxine Paetro)

The 5th Horseman (and Maxine Paetro)

4th of July (and Maxine Paetro)

3rd Degree (and Andrew Gross)

2nd Chance (and Andrew Gross)

1st to Die

OTHER BOOKS

You've Been Warned (and Howard Roughan)

The Quickie (and Michael Ledwidge)

Maximum Ride: Saving the World and Other Extreme Sports

Step on a Crack (and Michael Ledwidge)

Judge & Jury (and Andrew Gross)

Maximum Ride: School's Out — Forever

Beach Road (and Peter de Jonge)

Lifeguard (and Andrew Gross)

Maximum Ride: The Angel Experiment

Honeymoon (and Howard Roughan)

santaKid

Sam's Letters to Jennifer

The Lake House

The Jester (and Andrew Gross)

The Beach House (and Peter de Jonge)

Suzanne's Diary for Nicholas

Cradle and All

Black Friday

When the Wind Blows

See How They Run

Miracle on the 17th Green (and Peter de Jonge)

Hide & Seek

The Midnight Club

Season of the Machete

The Thomas Berryman Number

For previews of upcoming James Patterson novels and information about the author, visit www.jamespatterson.com.

JAMES PATTERSON

SEASON OF THE MACHETE

GC

GRAND CENTRAL
PUBLISHING

NEW YORK   BOSTON

Copyright © 1977, 1995 by James Patterson
All rights reserved. Except as permitted under the U.S. Copyright Act of 1976, no part of this publication may be reproduced, distributed, or transmitted in any form or by any means, or stored in a database or retrieval system, without the prior written permission of the publisher.

Cover design by Dale Fiorillo
Cover art by James Montalbano

Grand Central Publishing
Hachette Book Group
237 Park Avenue
New York, NY 10017
Visit our website at www.HachetteBookGroup.com

Grand Central Publishing is a division of Hachette Book Group, Inc.

The Grand Central Publishing name and logo is a trademark of Hachette Book Group, Inc.

Printed in the United States of America

Originally published in hardcover by Little, Brown and Company
First Paperback Printing: April 1995
Reissued: August 2006

33 32 31 30 29 28 27

April 30, 1980; Turtle Bay

On the gleaming white-sand lip of the next cove, Kingfish and the Cuban can see a couple walking on the beach. They are just stick figures at this distance. Absolutely perfect victims. *Perfect*.

Hidden in palm trees and sky blue wild lilies, the two killers cautiously watch the couple slowly come their way and disappear into the cove.

The Cuban wears a skull-tight, red-and-yellow bandanna; rip-kneed khaki trousers; scuffed, pale orange construction boots from the Army-Navy Store in Miami. The man called Kingfish has on nothing but greasy U.S. Army khakis.

The muscles of both men ripple in the hard, beating Caribbean sun.

The bright sun makes diamonds and blinking asterisks all over the sea. It glints off a sugar-cane machete hanging from the belt of the Cuban.

The weatherbeaten farm implement is two and a half feet long and sharp as a razor blade.

South of their hiding place, a great wrecked schooner—the *Isabelle Anne*—sits lonely and absurd, visited only by yellow birds and fish. Thirty yards farther south, the beach elbows around steep black rocks and makes a crystal path for walking. At this sharp bend lie reef fish, coral, sargassum, oyster drills, sea urchins.

Soon now, the two killers expect the couple to emerge from the cove and reappear on the narrow white path. The victims.

Perhaps a dark, bejeweled prime minister up on holiday from South America? Or an American politician with a coin- and milk-fed young woman who was both secretary and mistress?

Someone worth their considerable fees and passage to this serene and beautiful part of the world. Someone worth $50,000 apiece for less than one week's work.

Instead, a harmless-looking pair of adolescents turn the seaweed-strewn bend into Turtle Bay.

A bony, long-haired rich boy. A white-blond girl in a *Club Mediterranee* T-shirt. Americans.

On the run, they clumsily get out of their shirts, shorts, sandals, and underwear. Balls and little tits naked, they shout something about last one in is a rotten egg and run into the low, starry waves.

Twenty or thirty feet over their heads, seagulls make a sound almost like mountain sheep bleating.

Aaaaaa! Aaaaaa! Aaaaaa! Aaaaaa!

The man called Kingfish puts out an expensive black cigar in the sand. A low, animal moan rises out of his throat.

"We couldn't have come all this way to kill these two little shits."

The Cuban cautions him, "Wait and see. Watch them carefully."

"Aaagghh! Aaagghh!" The boy offers tin-ear bird imitations from the rippling water.

The slender blond girl screams, "I can't stand it. It's so goddamn unbelievably beautiful!"

She dives into sparkling aquamarine waves. Surfaces with her long hair plastered against her head. Her white breasts are small, nubby; up-pointed and rubbery from the cool water.

"I love this place already. Don't *ever* want to go back. Gramercy Park—*yeck!* I spit on East Twenty-third Street. Yeck! Yahoo! Yow!"

The Cuban slowly raises his hand above the blue lilies and prickle bushes. He waves in the direction of a green sedan parked on a lush hill overlooking the beach.

The sedan's horn sounds once. Their signal.

An eerie silence has come over the place.

Heartbeats; surf; little else.

The boy and girl lie on fluffy beach towels to dry under the sun. They close their eyes, and the backs of their eyelids become kaleidoscopes of changing color.

The girl sings, " 'Eastern's got my sunshine . . . ' "

The boy makes an impolite gurgling sound.

As the girl opens one eye, she feels a hard slap on the top of her head. It is painfully hot all of a sudden, and she feels dizzy. She starts to say *"Aahhh"* but chokes on thick, bubbling blood.

Pop . . . pop . . .

The slightest rifle shots echo in the surrounding hills.

Bullets travel out of an expensive West German rifle at 3,300 feet per second.

Then Kingfish and the Cuban come and stand over the bodies on the blood-spotted towels. Kingfish touches the boy's cheek and produces an unexpected moan, almost a growl.

"I don't think I like Mr. Damian Rose," he says in a soft, French-accented voice. "Very sorry I left Paris now. He's let this one live . . . for us."

The dying nineteen-year-old coughs. Blue eyes rolling, he speaks. "Why?" the boy asks. "Didn't do anything. . . ."

The Cuban swings the machete high. He chops

down as if he were in the thickest jungle brush, as if he were cutting a tree with a single stroke.

Chop, wriggle, lift.

The killer meticulously attacks both bodies with the long broadsword. Clean, hard strokes. Devastating. Blood squirts high and sprays the killer. Flesh and bone part like air in the path of the razor-sharp knife. Puddles of frothy blood are quickly soaked up by the sand, leaving dark red stains.

When the butchering is over, the Cuban drives the machete deep into the sand. He sets a red wool hat over the knife's handle and hasp.

Then both killers look up into the hills. They see the distant figure of Damian Rose beside the shiny green car. The handsome blond man is motioning for them to hurry back. He is waving his fancy German rifle high over his head.

What they can't quite see is that Damian Rose is smiling in triumph.

THE PREFACE

The Damian and Carrie Rose Diary

> Consider the raw power and unlimited
> potential of the good old-fashioned "thrill
> kill." Under proper supervision, of course.
>
> The Rose Diary

January 23, 1981; New York City

At 6:30 A.M. on the twenty-third of January, the birth date of his only child, Mary Ellen, Bernard Siegel—tall, dark, slightly myopic—began his "usual" breakfast of loose scrambled eggs, poppy-seed bagel, and black coffee at Wolf's Delicatessen on West Fifty-seventh Street in New York City.

After the satisfying meal, Siegel took a Checker cab through slushy brown snow to 800 Third Avenue. He used his private collection of seven keys to let himself into the modern dark-glass building, then into the offices of the publisher par excellence for whom he worked, and finally into the largest *small* office on that floor—his office—to try to get some busywork done before the many-too-many phones began to ring; to try to get home early enough to spend time with his daughter. On her twelfth birthday.

A young woman, very, very tan, squeaky clean, with premature silver all through her long, sandy hair, was standing before the dark, double-glazed windows.

The woman appeared to be watching 777 Third Avenue (the building across and down Third Avenue), or perhaps she was just staring at her own reflection.

Bernard Siegel said, "One—how the hell did you get in here? Two—who the hell are you? Three—please leave."

"My name is Carrie Rose." The woman turned to face him. She looked to be twenty-eight or twenty-nine, spectacularly poised and cool.

"I've come to make you an even more famous man than you are now. You are Siegel, aren't you?"

The editor couldn't hold back a slight smile, the smallest possible parting of thin, severe lips. She called him "Siegel."

Damn these shameless, impudent young writers, he thought. Had she actually *slept* in his office to get an interview? To give lucky him first crack at this year's *Fear of Flying*, or *Flying*, or *The Flies*?

Squinting badly, pathetically, for a man under forty, Siegel studied Carrie Rose. *Mrs.* Carrie Rose, he was to find out soon. Wife of Damian Rose. Soldier of fortune herself.

Under closer scrutiny, the young woman was striking, tall, and fashionably trim. *Vogue*-ish.

She had on large tortoiseshell eyeglasses that made her look more sharp-witted than she probably was; the blue pin-striped suit was meant to keep Siegel off his guard, he was sure. An old Indian dodge.

"All right, I'm Siegel," the nearsighted editor finally admitted. "I'm hardly famous. And this sort of clever, gratuitous nonsense doesn't cut it with me. . . . Please leave my office. Go back and write one more draft of your wonderful book. Make a regular-hours appointment with my—"

"Oh, but you are famous, Bernard." The woman interrupted him with an ingenue's toothy grin. "You're so well known, in fact, that busy people like myself go to great inconvenience to *give* you million-dollar book properties. Books that will make, at the very least, *dents* in history."

Siegel laughed. A cruel little laugh, but she deserved it.

"Only a million for it?"

Carrie Rose laughed, too. "Something like that."

She examined Siegel closely, then looked casu-

ally around his office at the unmatched oak and pine
bookcases on two of the walls; an Olivetti Lettera
typewriter tucked inside the banged-up rolltop desk,
with sheafs of crisp white bond stacked neatly beside it; new, shiny book jackets pinned to a cork
board; manuscripts in different-color typewriter-pa-
per boxes.

The editor.

Siegel put down his briefcase, kicked off his loafers, and sat on his chair. He gave her a long cold
stare. "Well, where is this magnum opus?"

"You haven't had it ghostwritten yet," the young
woman said. *Carrie Rose.* "Your writer's source
material will be a diary my husband, Damian, and
I kept last year. An unusual, very original diary that
will cost you *two* million dollars. It's about . . . an
awful nest of machete murders. Over a hundred of
them."

The pretty woman said it very coolly . . . "an
awful nest of machete murders."

PART 1

The Season of the
Machete

March–July, 1979
Death in
Lathrop Wells

.

CHAPTER ONE

Damian theorized that within fifty years
man would move onto and into the sea.
San Dominica was only a very small
beginning. An exploratory expedition. Kid
stuff. The people who engineered it didn't
understand their own inner motivation . . .
three-fifths of the world is water, and that
was about to be fought over on a
staggering scale. . . .

The Rose Diary

February 24, 1979; Lathrop Wells, Nevada

As the stupid, piggy Chevrolet Impala floated
through buzzard-infested desert, Isadore "the
Mensch" Goldman was thinking that he was
slightly surprised there really was a *state* of Nevada.

Every so often, though, the Chevrolet passed a tin
road sign with PROPERTY OF THE STATE OF NEVADA

stamped into it by some convict at Washoe County Jail.

Once, Goldman even saw some Nevadans: a woman and small children with frayed ankle boots, turquoise jewelry, faces the color of pretzel sticks.

Somewhere out here they tested H-bombs, the old man was thinking. At Mercury, Nevada.

Then the seventy-four-year-old's mind went walking.

He remembered something itchy about the still-not-to-be-believed Bay of Pigs invasion. Then a very brief, fuzzy association he'd had with Rafael Trujillo that same year: 1961.

Goldman's *history*. All leading up to February 24, 1979. The biggest day of the old man's life.

Maybe.

A man named Vincent "Zio" Tuch was patting Isadore's gray-striped banker's trousers at one baggy knee. Death spots were all over Tuch's unsteady hand.

"Bizee Izzee, what are you thinkin'?" Tuch rasped. "You thinkin' this is a big-fashion setup, Izzie? That's what I'm thinkin'."

"Aahh . . . I'm getting too damn old to think all the time." The consigliere casually dismissed the powerful old capo. It was a typically stupid, if well-meant, Mustache Pete question.

Old Tuch told him to go make shit in his own pants—which was also typical.

Also typical was the fact that the *caporegime* smelled of cheap hair tonic spilled over twenty-year-old dandruff.

Goldman had flatly predicted that the final meeting at Lathrop Wells would be ridiculous beyond human belief. Even he was surprised. It had the *consistency* of Silly Putty. It looked like the opening scene of an Alfred Hitchcock movie.

To begin with, both sides arrived at the farm in the most absurd "anonymous-looking" automobiles.

Goldman watched and counted bodies through the green-tinted windows of his own Impala.

There were nine chauffeurs driving such cars as Mustangs, Wildcats, Hornets, Cougars—even a Volkswagen Beetle.

There were seven bodyguards, out-and-out Buster Crabbe types.

Eleven actual participants besides himself and the shriveling zombie Tuch.

Somebody had remarked at the last meeting that they didn't want to have another Appalachia at Lathrop Wells: twenty Cadillac Fleetwoods suddenly arriving at some deserted farmhouse. Drawing attention from locals or the state police.

So there were none of the usual big black cars at the meeting in the Nevada desert.

All of the twenty-seven men wore dark business suits, with the exception of one Gucci-Pucci fag and Frankie "the Cat" Rao of Brooklyn, New York. Rao wore a black-and-white-checked sports jacket, a sleazy open-necked electric blue shirt, white Bing Crosby shoes.

"Dirty azzhole," old Tuch said. "Azzhole with all of his pinky rings."

"All very predictable," Isadore Goldman muttered. The old man lit up his first cigarette in more than eight months. Then he headed inside, through hot, heavy air that smelled like horses.

Inside the farmhouse it was air-conditioned, thank God.

A Fedders was blowing dust and what looked like cereal flakes all around the rustic, low-ceilinged rooms.

Goldman noticed the other side's head man whisper something to a younger man—his aide-de-camp. The younger man looked a little like the Hollywood actor Montgomery Clift.

His name was Brooks Campbell, and he would be going to the Caribbean for them.

The older man, their side's main spokesman, was Harold Hill. Harry the Hack to the trade.

Harold Hill had spent nearly ten years in Southeast Asia, and he had a certain inscrutable look about him. Something intangible. Isadore Goldman suspected that Hill was a pretty good killer for such an obvious loser type.

Within ten minutes the thirteen important negotiators had settled down comfortably around a wide-beam table in the living room. Characteristically, they had taken opposite sides at the big wooden table.

Dark, slightly European-looking men on one side.

All-American football-player types on the other.

"By way of a brief introduction"—Goldman began the meeting after allowing just a snitch of small talk—"it was agreed at the last meeting—January seventeenth—that if Damian and Carrie Rose were available, they would be satisfactory contract operators for everybody concerned. . . ."

Goldman peeked over his silver-rimmed eyeglasses. So far, no objections.

"Consequently," he continued, "the Roses were contacted at a hotel in Paris. The St. Louis, it's called. An old gun sellers' hangout through several wars now.

"The Roses were given one month to prepare an outline for a plan that would achieve results agreeable to both sides at this table. They declined making an appearance at this meeting, however."

The *consigliere* looked up again. He then began to read from twenty-odd pages sent to him by the Roses. The pages outlined two rough plans for the proposed operations. One plan was titled "Systematic Government Assassinations," the other was simply called "Machete."

Also included in the brief was a list of pros and cons for each plan.

In fact, what seemed to impress both sides gathered around the table—what had impressed Goldman himself—was the seriousness with which both theoretical plans had been approached and researched.

They were referred to specifically as "rough," "experimental," but the outline for each seemed obsessively airtight. Typically Damian Rose.

"The final bid they put in for this work," Isadore Goldman reported, "is one point two million. I myself think it's a fair estimate. I think it's low, in fact. . . . I also think this man Damian Rose is a genius. Perhaps the woman is, too. Gentlemen?"

Predictably, Frankie Rao had the first word on the plans.

"Is that fuckin' francs or dollars, Izzie?" he shouted down the wooden plank table. "It's fuckin' dollars those loonie tunes are talking about, isn't it?"

Goldman noticed that their man, Harold Hill, seemed startled and upset by the New York mobster.

The young man who looked like Montgomery Clift broke into a toothpaste smile, however. *Brooks Campbell.* Good for you, Isadore Goldman thought. Smart boy. Break the goddamn tensions down a little.

For the first time since the meeting began, most

of the men at the long wooden table laughed. Both sides laughed like hell. Even Frankie Rao began to howl.

As the laughter died down, Goldman nodded to a dark-haired man who sat very quietly at the far end of the table. Goldman then nodded at their side's chief man, Harold Hill.

"Does the figure include all expenses?" was Hill's only question. The young man at his side, Campbell, nodded as if this were his question, too.

"It includes every expense," Isadore Goldman said. "The Roses expect this to take approximately one year to carry out. They'll have to use twenty to thirty other professionals along the way. A *Who's Who* of the most elite mercenaries."

"Dirt cheap." The quiet, dark-haired man suddenly spoke in a deep, Senate floor voice. The man was Charles Forlenza, forty-three-year-old don of the Forlenza Family. The boss of bosses.

"You've gotten us a good price and good people, Isadore. As I expected. . . . I can't speak for Mr. Hill, but I'm pleased with this work myself."

"The price is appropriate for this kind of guerrilla operation." Harold Hill addressed the don. "The Roses' reputation for this sort of complex, delicate work is excellent. I'm happy. Good."

At this point on February 24, 1979, the United States, through a proprietary company called Great Western Air Transport, entered into one of the more

interesting alliances in its two-hundred-year history:
a large-scale working agreement with the Charles
Forlenza Family of the West Coast. The Cosa Nostra.

For both sides it meant that they could immediately farm out some very necessary dirty work.

Neither the United States nor the Forlenzas
wanted to soil their hands with what had to be done
in the Caribbean during 1979.

That was why they had so very carefully sought
out Damian and Carrie Rose. *Les Dements*, as the
couple was once called in Southeast Asia. The Maniacs.

Two hours after the meeting in southwestern Nevada—on the way back to Las Vegas—a silver-gray Buick Wildcat stopped along a long stretch of
flat, open highway. The youthful chauffeur of the
car got out. He went to the back door of the sedan
and opened it. Then Melo Russo politely asked his
boss to get out of the car.

"Who the fuck do you think you're talking to?"
Frankie Rao said to his driver, a skinny young shark
in reflector sunglasses.

"All right, so fuck you, then," Melo said.

He fired three times into the backseat of the Buick. Blood spattered all over the rear windows and
slowly misted down onto the light silver seat covers.
Then Russo dragged Frankie the Cat's body outside
and put it in the trunk of the car.

It had been quietly decided at the farmhouse meeting that Frankie Rao was an unacceptable risk for Harold Hill and the nice young man who looked like Montgomery Clift.

"Typical," Isadore Goldman muttered somewhere out on the Nevada desert.

CHAPTER TWO

Once—in France, this was—in June or July—Damian had gone on a tirade about how perfect our work in Cambodia and Vietnam had been. How it bothered the hell out of him that no one could know. That there was no way to capitalize on the work . . . <u>Funny quirk (twist)</u>: In a French village, Grasse, we sat in an espresso house. Damian conversed in English with a very polite street cleaner who spoke no English at all. He told the man every last detail about the Caribbean adventure. "Genie! Demon! <u>Non?</u>" he said in French at the end of it. The poor confused street cleaner smiled as if Damian were an insane little boy. . . .

                                    The Rose Diary

June 11, 1979; Paris

Three months after the Nevada meeting, in the fashionable St.-Germain section of Paris, Damian Rose swung back and forth on a rope hammock from Au Printemps. The hammock was tied to a heavy stonework terrace. The large pigeon-gray terrace overlooked the Jardin des Tuileries, the Seine, the Louvre. The scenery of Paris was as pretty as a Seurat painting this hazy morning.

Lying there in the late spring sun, Rose indulged himself in his one fatuous addiction: the reading of sensationalist newspapers and magazines.

After perusing *The Boys from Brazil*, then glancing at the opening stories in the *Enquirer*, the overseas edition of *Time* magazine, and *Soldier of Fortune*, the elegant man rolled out of the hammock. Inside his and Carrie's apartment, he got out of a lamb's-wool pullover and expensive cream gabardines. Then he started to piece together the international costume of American students abroad.

He put on faded blue jeans, a police blue workshirt, lop-heeled Frye boots, and, finally, a red cowboy neckerchief. He applied light makeup to his eyes. Fitted a long dark wig over his own shorter hair.

Today Damian Rose was going to play the part of a professor from the Sorbonne.

He had to buy a small supply of drugs in Les Halles: amphetamines, cocaine, Thai sticks. Then off to meet with a mercenary soldier who called himself the Cuban.

Tucking the workshirt tightly into Jockey shorts and zipping up his jeans, Damian walked through a living room overflowing with Broadway and Haymarket theater paraphernalia.

Then out the apartment's front door with a bang.

"Bonjour," he said to an *emmerdeuse* named Marie, an ancient woman who was always reading newspapers in the light of the hallway window.

Then boots clomped down marble stairs to a circular courtyard inside the building itself.

Damian climbed into a small black convertible in the courtyard. He left the convertible's top up. Windows partially up. Visors down. He put on blue air force–style sunglasses.

The sports car rolled out of the yard's black ironwork gates, and Rose started to hum an old song he liked very much—sweet "Lili Marlene."

It was a brilliantly clear and warm spring day now. White as paper.

The sweet smell of French bread baking filled the air on the narrow side streets.

As the shiny black car turned onto the boulevard St.-Germain, a bicyclist—a healthy-looking girl in an oatmeal tank top—strained her long, swanlike neck to see the face of the young man behind the sun-dappled windshield.

The pretty girl wasn't quite fast enough.

As of June 1979, no one who shouldn't would know what the face of Damian Rose looked like.

April 24, 1979, Tuesday
Machete
3
Guilty!

CHAPTER THREE

Bookkeeping . . . over the course of the year, we had to hire over a hundred different people. We paid out nearly $600,000 in overhead expenses. We paid forgers from Brussels, counterfeiters, gun salesmen from East Germany and the United States, informers, dope peddlers, whores, pickpockets, American intelligence men, top mercenaries like Kingfish Toone, Blinkie Tomas (the Cuban), Clive Lawson. And not one of these people was ever told exactly what it was that we were putting together in the Caribbean. . . .

The Rose Diary

The saying "Mad dogs and Englishmen" refers obliquely to the fact that our sun will cook you like bacon. Beware!

Sign on beach at Turtle Bay

April 24, 1979; Coastown, San Dominica

Tuesday. The First Day of the Season.

Not by coincidence, April 24 marked the end of the most spectacularly newsworthy trial ever held on the eighty-one-by-thirty-nine-mile Caribbean island of San Dominica.

Parts of the pyrotechnic high court scene were hard to imagine or describe.

For a beginning, the tiny, plain courtroom was packed to its high, square beam rafters. The room was as noisy as a sporting event. The slow-turning fans on the ceiling, like the ones in the movie *Casablanca*, were a sharp contrast to the frenzied atmosphere. The most perversely interesting of the defendants was fifteen-year-old Leon Rachet.

The five-foot-six-inch teenager had a slate black, intelligent face that was at the same time piggy and cruel. He had long black cornbraids that were sopping wet all through the trial, dripping at the ends like frayed rope hanging in the rain.

Every five minutes the boy's grandmother, his guardian, punctuated the final proceedings with a loud, pitiful scream from her seat in the courtroom gallery. "Leon!" she shouted. "My bway Leon! Oh, no, son!"

"You are murdering curs without any shame." The seventy-year-old judge, Andre Dowdy, lectured the teenager and the two grown men standing beside him.

"I feel no mercy toward any of you. Not even toward you, boy. I consider you all mad dogs. . . ."

Flanking Rachet, thirty-year-old Franklin Smith aimlessly shifted his weight from one orange work-boot to the other; Chicki Holt—father of fourteen children by five women, the local newspaper liked to reprint with every new story on the trial—just stared up at the plain white ceiling and watched the slow fans. Frankly Chicki was bored.

Eight months earlier the same three men had stood outside a stammering Volkswagen Superbug one mile from the country town of New Burg. They'd robbed an American tourist, Francis Cichoski, a fireman from Waltham, Massachusetts, on a golfing vacation.

At the end of the broad-daylight holdup, one of the three blacks had knocked the white man down with the business side of a sugar-cane machete. The blow had killed Cichoski instantly. Then the man's crew-cut head had been chopped off and left lying on its cheek on the blacktop road.

In the eight months that followed, the motivation for the murder had been described as racial unrest; economic unrest; sex unrest; blood lust; obeah; soul music and kinky reggae; insanity; and, finally, the unsubtle beginning of a terrifying Pan-Caribbean revolution. These were not mutually exclusive, it was understood.

Recently, however, San Dominican's prime minister, Joe Walthey, had simplified the sociological aspects of the crime.

"No matter what else," the dictatorial black said over rolling, blipping island TV, "these men must hang, or this island shall never find peace with itself again. Mark my words on this.

"The life of Francis Cichoski must be avenged," Walthey repeated three times before he finally faded from the television screen.

At 10:30 A.M. Judge Andre Dowdy read his verdict in an unsteady, emotion-packed voice.

"All three of you men—Franklin Smith, Donald 'Chicki' Holt, Leon Elmore Rachet," he read, "are found guilty of the murder as presented in evidence before me and this court. All of you will be taken to the Russville jail, and there be hanged no more than one week from today. May God have mercy on your souls. And on my own."

"An' on yo' ahss, too!" young Leon Rachet suddenly screamed out in the hushed courtroom. "An' on yo' ahss, Dowdy mon."

Franklin Smith turned to the teenager, winced, and said, "Oohh, Leon, mon."

At 10:40 the dull gray roof of the Potts Rum Factory blew off like a slapstick comedian's hat;

then flashes of leaping flames of orange and red fired up into the balmy clear blue sky.

Literally within minutes, the Coastown factory was gone; an entire block of the capital was hopelessly ablaze.

At precisely 11:00 two white foremen were beaten senseless with ball bats at the Cow Park Bauxite Mines.

A hundred car windows were smashed in an executive parking lot.

The executive dining room was rushed, and all the prime ribs and hot fried chicken were either taken away or destroyed.

Inside the courtroom in Coastown, meanwhile, Franklin Smith and Chicki Holt screamed obscenely at Judge Dowdy. Their already hoarse, long-haired American lawyer screamed at the elderly judge, too. They called him "mama's man"; "runny ass"; "shit pussy"; "blood clot."

Young Leon Rachet stood by quietly, simply watching. He reached inside his back pocket and produced a black beret for his sweaty head. At fifteen he fancied himself part Huey P. Newton, part Selassie, part Che.

During the mad courtroom screaming, he turned to Franklin Smith and told the older man to shut his "black nager-boy mout."

Strangely, the thirty-year-old man did as he was told.

Outside the cigar-box courthouse, the reggae singer Bob Marley was being blasted from loudspeakers on top of a rainbow-colored VW van.

Marley and his Wailers also yelled out of oversize transistor radios along the crowded palm-tree-lined sidewalks.

Angry black faces screamed at the courthouse building as if it were alive. Rude boys in the crowd carried posters promoting the cause of the revolutionary colonel Monkey Dred, and also of His Imperial Majesty Haile Selassie. Pretty, innocent-faced schoolchildren waved beautiful hand-painted banners—GO HOME ADMIRAL NELSON; GO HOME LAURENCE ROCKEFELLER; SAN DOMINICA A BLACK REPUBLIC.

Shiny-faced city policemen marched up Court Street behind see-through riot shields. People threw ripe fruit at the police. Mangoes, green coconuts, small melons.

A nut-skinned man in army fatigues ran up to a TV camera and made a bizarre, contorted face into the lens. "Aaahh deangerous!" he shouted, and became famous across the world.

At 11:15 a row of five Hertz rentals was blown up with plastique at Robert F. Kennedy Airport outside Coastown.

At 11:30 the three black murderers were led out onto the shiny white courthouse porch.

The San Dominican terrors were about to begin in earnest.

Fifteen-year-old Leon Rachet had on a Day-Glo flowered shirt and dark Tonton Macoute sunglasses. His black beret was tipped slightly over one eye. Deangerously.

At first Rachet smiled broadly as he waved his handcuffed hands high over his head like a prizefight winner. Then, as the police shoved him down the glaring white steps, the boy began literally to scream at the sky.

"Dred kill yo', mon! Monkey kill al you'! Slit al yo' troats." Over and over the boy screamed out the name of an island revolutionary.

"Monkey Dred slit me own auntie's troat. Ay-ee! Ay-ee!"

Suddenly a well-dressed black man in the crowd screamed out above all the other noise. "Gee-zass, mon. Oh, Gee-zass Ky-rist!"

Someone had thrown a sun-catching, silver Frisbee high up into the air. It curved down into the crowd around the handcuffed murderers.

As fifteen-year-old Leon Rachet reached the bottom of the courthouse steps, where the back door of a black police Rover was flung open to receive him, his eyes turned up toward the suddenly descending silver Frisbee—and a white man in a Panama suit and hat stepped out of the crowd and fired three shots into the mad boy's face.

Carrie Rose watched the strange, possessed teenager crumple up and fall. She was among the large group of white tourists behind police lines. She hoped the rest of the terrors would go as smoothly as this one had.

Robert F. Kennedy Airport; Coastown, San Dominica

Tuesday Evening.

At 9:45 that night, an American Airlines Boeing 727 began its light, feathery approach down into San Dominica's Robert F. Kennedy Airport.

The massive silver plane glided in amazingly low over the blue-black Caribbean.

Big red lights blinked at one-second intervals on the plane's wings and tail. The red lights reflected beautifully off the dark blue sea.

Hidden in blackness beside a filling station near runway two, Damian Rose watched the pretty landing with considerable interest. He ran through his final plan one more time.

Meanwhile, out on runway one, the tires of the 727 were already touching down with the slightest bump and grind. A half-stoned calypso band began to play up near the main terminal.

The airplane's wheels screeched as its brakes and thrust-reversal system took hold.

As the plane reached a point halfway to its landing mark, Damian Rose was forced to make a decision. Raising an expensive German-made rifle to his cheek, he got a small dark box on the runway into the clear greenish light of his nightscope.

He fired three times.

The unsophisticated bomb on the runway went off, drowning out the rifle explosions, and blew away a large section of the airplane's belly.

As the 727 rolled to a stop, flames burst from its midsection, then out the windows over its wings.

Doors flew open, and emergency escape equipment tumbled outside. Screaming passengers started to come out of the airplane, some of them on fire.

The airport's two emergency trucks headed out toward the burning plane, slowly at first, their inexperienced drivers not believing what they were seeing.

A person's burning head was in one of the plane's tiny windows.

A white woman on fire ran across the dark tarmac, looking like a burning cross.

A stewardess stood at one door with her fingers buried in her frosted blond hair, screaming for help.

Four hours later—when the fire was finally out—

six people from the 727 were dead, more than fifty others had been burned, and nobody on the island had a clue why it happened.

The next day the puzzle seemed to become a bit clearer.

April 25, 1979,
Wednesday
Couple
Slain
On
Beach

Chapter Four

In 1967, when we were selling fifty- and
hundred-milligram bags of heroin,
Damian told me that he aspired to be the
greatest criminal mind in the world. He
said that the world was ripe for a criminal
hero: brilliant, with a little raffish touch of
William Henry Bonney—a little Butch
Cassidy gilding. . . . I liked that idea very
much. I got to be Katharine Ross in the
fantasy.

The Rose Diary

April 25, 1979; Turtle Bay, San Dominica

*Wednesday Afternoon. The Second Day of the
Season*

On the macadam highway that sliced through
Turtle Bay, Peter Macdonald—a young man who

was to play a large part in things to come—made his daily bicycle ride through the lush, sun-streaked paradise.

As he pedaled a ten-speed Peugeot, Macdonald was enjoying the extra luxury of recalling several foolish glories out of his past.

Nearly twenty-nine years old, Peter rode well enough. He looked healthy. Physically he was an attention getter. A pleasantly muscular six feet one, he rode in holey gray gym shorts with *Property of USMA West Point* printed in gold on one leg.

He wore ragged Converse All-Star sneakers from Herman Spiegel's Sportin' Supplies in Grand Rapids, Michigan . . . gray-and-red Snowbird socks that made his feet peel their yellowing calluses . . . a bent, dusty *Detroit Tigers* souvenir hat that looked as if it had been worn every day of his life. And nearly had been.

Underneath the baseball hat, his chestnut-colored hair was cut short, very high up on the sides. It was a real throwback haircut—a cut they used to call a "West Pointer."

Nearly everything about Peter Macdonald was throwback: his young lumberjack's good looks; his high Episcopal morals, philosophies; midwestern farmer stubbornness. Everything except for the last four months, anyway—the times he'd spent on San Dominica—the four months he'd been a lackey bartender, a beachcomber, a fornicator. Quite frankly, a nothing.

As he passed through the island hills, gnats began to swim in the sweat on his strong back.

Peter the Ridiculous, his girlfriend, Jane Cooke, liked to say in private places.

Once upon a time Peter had run around Michigan like that: quietly, desperately, ridiculously . . . in winter . . . in ten-pound black rubber sea boots.

Once upon a time he'd been an army brat—the last of the six Macdonald brothers, the last of the Super Six; then he'd been a West Point cadet; then a Special Forces sergeant in Vietnam and Cambodia.

Old foolish glories.

When the high weeds and banana plants started to get too thick—buggy, disturbingly itchy—Peter rode closer to the sea, on the wrong side of the two-lane Shore Highway. He was getting tired now. Rhythm going all to hell. Breaking down. Paradise Lost.

He looked down on the starry Caribbean—Turtle Bay—and thought that he would take a swim after his ride. Find Jane and take a dip with her . . . maybe talk her into spending the afternoon in bed.

He was very, very tired now, though. Knees threatened to wipe out his chin. Pedals fell flat as pancakes.

Stik-shhh, stik-shhh, stik-shhh, stik-shhh . . .

Shiny with sweat, Peter came around a sharp

bend in the highway . . . and saw Damian Rose . . . thirty yards ahead of him on the road.

The tall blond man stood with a rifle in the crook of his arm, looking out over the sea.

Peter's first thought was that the blond man was enjoying some impromptu hunting. Pigs, most likely.

He could see the man's car parked a little way up the road. Green sedan. License plate CY and a few numbers.

Local? . . . Hadn't seen him around. . . . Must be renting a villa. . . . Looked rich enough. Snobby, too. . . .

For some reason Peter took the man to be an Englishman. . . . He saw the flash of a tag marked "Harrods" inside the man's jacket. . . . The tall blond Englishman. Smashing.

As he passed by, the blond man turned and yelled out to him. Almost as if he'd been in a trance.

He yelled "Constitutional!" Some long word. . . .

Macdonald took it for a greeting. Waved. Kept riding.

He even picked up his speed a little. The slightest show-off move: Daniel Morelon imitation. That saved him, they said.

The whole scene took less than fifteen seconds. Fifteen mind-bending, life-changing seconds.

Then, another turn down the Shore Highway—

bicycle flew downhill like a bat whistling—Peter was startled by a loud thrashing in the kelly green bush leading down to the beach.

He expected a little band of goats or some wild pigs. What he saw were two sweating, barebacked blacks running up the hill.

One of the men, the Cuban, was covered with blood. Smears that looked like finger paints.

All of which would eventually send tremendous shock waves through the CIA, the Cosa Nostra, the San Dominican government. . . . At a cost of one and a quarter million dollars, the Roses weren't supposed to leave witnesses.

As for Peter Macdonald, he was in deep trouble . . . but at least he was on the run.

CHAPTER FIVE

In Paris, he would sleep no more than three or four hours during the months before we left for the Caribbean. Usually, he'd go to bed around five in the morning. Until then, he'd just be sitting in front of a gooseneck lamp, turned so the bright light was almost shining in his face. Thinking things through. He'd sleep three or four hours, then be up by nine at the latest. Thinking some more about the machetes.

The Rose Diary

Michael O'Mara and his wife, Faye, were walking very, very slowly.

Sand worshipers, they plodded westward, from cove to shining cove.

Sixty-year-old Faye hummed absently to herself. She made up a silly tune for "She sells seashells by the seashore."

From a distance, Mike and Faye looked like two old men down on the beach . . . as they turned a sharp bend and entered Turtle Bay.

"No wonder I'm so damn achy and tired," Mike said, hitching his baggy, electric blue swim trunks every fourth or fifth step, walking with his feet splayed out like a large arthritic duck.

"I can't sleep at these goddamn, ridiculous hotel prices. Who can sleep at forty . . . no. What is it? Fifty? . . . No, forty. Say *thirty* dollars every time you snooze. . . . I'll wait'll Coastown to sleep at those prices. At those prices, I'll wait'll we get back home if I have to."

Faye laughed right into the long ash of Mike's cigar. "That's very humorous, Miguel."

She stooped to pick up a nutmeg seashell, and her stomach bounced like a beach ball in her one-piece bathing suit. "Ha. Ha. Ha. That really cracks me up. Hee, hee. See, I'm laughing."

"Laugh away. Room in Coastown's thirty bucks for a double. European plan. That place I think I could sleep, maybe. Shit fire and save matches. Skip eatin' dinners altogether. Cut out the goat steaks easy enough. . . ."

Which part Faye didn't really hear—not this time around on the familiar broken, skipping record: Mike. Instead the big white-haired lady seemed annoyed at the shell she'd just found.

"I hate some people." She weighed the tiny shell

scientifically in her palm. "The way they make ashtrays out of these beautiful things. Nature's wonders. Such a waste. And *sooo* tacky."

Mike O'Mara briefly examined his wife's new treasure. He thought he heard somebody coming and looked off toward the bushes. Nothing. Couldn't see worth a shit anymore.

He dropped her seashell in the rope net bag he was dragging along the hot sand. Began to feel a little like a Fairmount Park sanitation man, he thought. Asshole seashells.

"Who gets this work of art?" he asked in the seldom used, nonshouting voice he used as "good old Mike," doorman and purveyor of goodwill at the Rittenhouse Club in Philadelphia.

"That one goes to Libby Gibbs." Faye stooped for another shell, a rose murex, she thought. "Uhnn . . . which leaves Aunt Betsy, Bobo, Yacky. And Mama."

Mike stooped down and splashed cool water around his ankles. Pink, swollen, starting-to-blister ankles. Damn. Jaysus Christ Almighty. Was he actually paying good money to be tortured like this?

When he straightened up, he took his wife's soft, flabby upper arm. Dammit, he owed her this trip. He really did. Second honeymoon? Whatever you wanted to call it.

"Faye Wray," he said. "It's just that I don't understand why we have to fly away to some island. . . . Then buy presents for everybody and their brother. . . . Now if this was the Christmas Islands . . .''

Suddenly Faye O'Mara looked awfully sad and tired. She was thinking that her kids didn't care anymore. Mike certainly didn't care. Nobody in this big wide world cared a whit what she thought about anything.

"Aren't you having fun here, Mike?" she asked for real. Serious. Then the bucktoothed Irishwoman grinned—the eternal struggle between the two of them—sharing that . . . *something* . . . making her smile and feel tender toward Mike.

The answer to her question never came, though.

Because Mike O'Mara was running for the first time in fifteen years. Huffing and puffing forward, looking as if his knees were locked.

He couldn't believe his eyes and waved for Faye to stay back. "Go back, Faye. Go back."

The Philadelphia doorman had found a bloody machete driven halfway to China in the sand. He'd found the two hippies who had been killed and mutilated by the Cuban and Kingfish Toone.

And so had a hungry band of wild goats.

CHAPTER SIX

We forget that policemen are relatively
simple-minded human beings for the
most part. Damian said that they are
basically unequipped to deal with the
creative personality (criminal). It's
impossible for them now, and it's getting
worse. An amoral generation is coming up
fast. Can another police state be far
behind?

The Rose Diary

Wednesday Evening

It was getting dark fast, black and blue and pink
out over the Caribbean, when the chief of San Dominica's police force came to see the extraordinary
machete murders.

Twenty or so less important policemen and army
officials had already arrived. They were deployed
all over the beach, like survey engineers.

Taking notes. Making measurements. Spreading out litters and yellow sheets that looked like rain slickers from a distance.

The policemen's white pith helmets floated through the crowd like carnival balloons.

Before he did anything else, the chief of police counted the valuable helmets on the heads of his men.

Then Dr. Meral Johnson quietly pushed himself through a buzzing ring of bathing suits and cutoff blue jeans; bald heads and brown freckled decolletage; double-knit leisure suits and pantsuits and flowing Empire dresses.

At least four hundred very frightened and very confused vacationers had gathered on the finger-cove beach.

To get a look at the bodies.

And then not to believe their own eyes; not to believe their luck.

Once he was inside the circus of people, Dr. Johnson stopped to catch his breath. He lit up a stumpy black Albertson pipe. *Pup, pup, pup, pup . . .*

The Americans were restless tonight! He made a small joke, then quickly felt very bad about it. Very bad. Awful.

A little shorter than five feet ten, four-eyed, seer-suckered, two hundred fifty pounds, Meral Johnson looked rather tenuous as a policeman, he knew. Tenuous, or was it timorous?

More like a proper, stern West Indian schoolmaster—which he'd been—than a Joseph Wambaugh–style policeman come to solve grisly murders. More like a hick islander who polished his shoes with palm oil, his teeth with baking soda.

Well, so be it, Meral Johnson thought to himself. So be it. The massive policeman thereupon entered the machete Terrors.

Almost instantly the flustered German manager of the nearby Plantation Inn began to shout at him.

"What took you so long? Now you stop to smoke a pipe?"

Dr. Johnson paid the hotel manager as much attention as he would some sandfly buzzing around his trousers cuffs. Speaking to none of his subordinates first, he began to walk around the yellow rubber sheets that covered bits and pieces of the teenagers' bodies.

After his short walk, the police chief stood with his back to the sea and simply *watched* the scene of the double murder. He tried to bring his mind back down on an even keel.

The manager of the Plantation Inn had apparently ordered his waiters to cordon off the bodies of the two young people.

The waiters, mostly old blacks with fuzzy white crew cuts—earning less than thirty dollars a week—stood at parade-ground attention in their stiff white dinner jackets. Each man had on black dress shoes with especially shiny toes. Each held a flaming torch removed from the inn's dining veranda. Each of the waiters looked sad and dignified and, above all, respectful of the terrible situation.

The scene was extraordinary—both colonial and primitive—and Johnson wanted to be certain he had it reproduced, burned into his optic nerve, before he began the thumb-screwing work ahead of him this night.

What a sight—tragedy, mystery. The worst he'd ever come upon.

First, Dr. Johnson approached the very inexperienced, frightened constable of Turtle Bay District.

Almost since he had arrived, twenty-eight-year-old Bobbie Valentine had been kneeling among the rubber sheets, looking like a mourner, looking as if he would be sick to his stomach.

Meral Johnson kneeled and spoke to the man in a clear, relatively clean, Oxbridge accent. No trace of island patois.

"What is your thought here, Bobbie?" he asked. A short pause, then he answered his own question. "I think Colonel Dred, perhaps. He's contacted the newspapers and claimed responsibility, at least."

Before the constable had a chance to agree or disagree, the German hotel manager spoke over both their heads.

"*I am* Maximilian Westerhuis," he announced with authority—almost titular emphasis. "I manage the Plantation Inn. These two dead . . ."

The large black policeman stood up faster than seemed possible. His dark eyes flashed. Looking convincingly nasty, Johnson said the first thing that entered his head.

"You wish to make a confession here?"

Westerhuis took a confused step backward. "Of course not. Confessions? . . . Don't be absurd with me. . . ."

"Then I am talking to this very good policeman now." Dr. Johnson's voice returned to its usual polite whisper. "Please wait for me, Mr. Westerhuis. On the far side of your service crew."

The inn manager, tall, white blond, said nothing further. He stalked off angrily.

"Nazi," Johnson muttered—an obvious idea that nonetheless went completely over the head of Constable Valentine. "I must do something about this crowd," Johnson said. "Something smart would be preferable."

Smoking his black pipe, the police chief started to walk from sheet to sheet again. Very gently he lifted the bulky rubber covers, then put them back exactly as they had been. It looked almost as if the policeman were checking on small sleeping children.

He stayed over the severed head of the young woman for what seemed like a very long time.

Shining a small pocket light on the bodies, he studied the bloody faces and skulls.

The crowd of hotel guests became silent as he worked. Every man and woman watched him, but the police chief never looked up. For the first time in hours, you could hear birds in the air at Turtle Bay; you could hear the sea lapping.

Finally, with his head still down, as respectful as the old black waiters, Dr. Johnson walked back to his constable.

He'd spent the previous ten minutes, the entire slow dance back through the mutilated bodies, simply trying to gain some confidence from this crowd. To give them the impression that he'd handled murders like this before.

Now, maybe, he could begin some kind of investigation.

Using his handkerchief, he started by wriggling the sugar-cane machete out of the sand. He held the sharp broadsword up to the light of the moon.

"Hmmm," he muttered out loud. "Make sure no one takes any souvenirs." He spoke in a lower voice to Constable Bobbie Valentine. "Americans like souvenirs of disaster. We learned at least that much at the airplane fire. . . .

"And one final thing, Bobbie. Will you spread this word for me? . . . If any of these men sell their hats as souvenirs, tell them they'll be selling pukka beads and seashells on the streets by this time tomorrow night. I counted sixteen hats coming down here!''

Coastown, San Dominica

At 7:45 the young man who looked like Montgomery Clift sat alone at a shadowy table on the veranda of the Coastown Princess Hotel.

As he sipped a Cutty Sark Scotch with Perrier water, he tapped his swizzle stick to the soft calypso beat of "Marianne." Brooks Campbell was starting to get nervous.

Small problem: He was afraid the other people on the patio were beginning to notice that he was sitting there all by his lonesome.

Slightly larger problem: His Afro-haired waiter was hassling him, trying to get him to leave so a bigger party could sit at the table.

Very large problem: Damian Rose was half an hour late for their first, presumably their only, face-to-face meeting.

Brooks Campbell didn't know all the details about Turtle Bay yet, but the general way the Roses worked was beginning to grate on his nerves. At first there were supposed to be only ten or twelve deaths on San Dominica, something like the 1973 uprisings on St. Croix. Now it looked as if it would be worse than that. Much worse. Rose was handling everything his own idiosyncratic way, and that was why Campbell had asked for the meeting. Demanded a meeting.

At 8:15 Damian Rose still hadn't appeared.

Campbell sat and watched a huge artificial waterfall dump endless gallons of water into an epic swimming pool directly below the patio. He watched couples in bathing suits as they wound their way along pretty paths lined with palm and casuarina trees.

The small combo was playing a reggae tune now—"The Harder They Come." Revolutionary music.

By 8:45 Brooks Campbell realized that he wasn't going to meet Damian Rose.

Campbell had a sneaking suspicion that no one was ever going to see the mysterious soldier of fortune.

At nine o'clock the handsome thirty-one-year-old paid his bar bill at the Princess. He walked the twelve blocks to the U.S. embassy; heard war drums in the air out on the streets. Back at the embassy, he was greeted with the most disturbing news of his career.

Someone had seen a tall blond man at Turtle Bay that afternoon.

Someone had finally seen the face of Damian Rose.

Turtle Bay, San Dominica

The field machete left in the sand at Turtle Bay was half scythe, half butcher's cleaver.

From the look of it, it had seen heavy use on a sugar plantation or in the West Hills jungle. The knife part was twenty-six inches long, four inches wide. Heavy-duty steel. The wooden handle was seven inches, warped, badly nicked, with big rivets like a kitchen carving knife. When it was held in one hand, the machete brought to mind cutlasses and sword fighting.

Sitting in the paperback library at the Plantation Inn, Dr. Meral Johnson examined the sharp knife for a long time.

He held it up close to a bright reading lamp. He whipped it through the air, cutting at shadows. Scary weapon. Johnson had personally seen a machete cut a goat in half at a swipe.

The weary policeman plopped down on an old morris chair in the library. He began to sort through some of the loose, contradictory details of the case . . . the Turtle Bay massacre. The American Airlines' plane that was bombed. The curious shooting of Leon Rachet.

Right then, the best Dr. Johnson figured he could do was concentrate on details that might lead him or the army to the island revolutionary Monkey Dred. He instructed his men to do the same in their investigations.

It was an honest but costly mistake—and one the Roses had counted on.

Policemen are relatively simple-minded human beings . . .

Witnesses.

A tennis pro and his wife from Saddle River, New Jersey, had seen a black hobo on the beach near the time of the machete murders.

An elderly Englishwoman saw a group of "unruly native boys" congregating in the royal palms just beyond the inn's main stretch of beach.

A couple from Georgia remembered seeing an old black man with some mangy goats on a rope leash.

A pretty eleven-year-old girl was brought to Dr. Johnson because she had a story, her mother said. The girl explained that around eight o'clock that evening, she'd locked herself in her mother's suite. Then she'd screamed bloody murder until one of the hotel bartenders—Peter Macdonald—came and broke down the door with a fire ax. The girl's mother, an actress, wanted the police chief to get both of them on an airplane back to New York that evening. Crying, occasionally screaming at the black man, she said that her daughter was about to have a nervous breakdown.

Simultaneously, another group of "witnesses" was being questioned inside the inn's main business office.

"You're one of the bartenders here." Constable Bobbie Valentine spoke softly at first. The country policeman was sitting behind a Royal office typewriter, only occasionally glancing up from his notepad. "Talk to me, mon."

In as few words as possible, Peter Macdonald tried to explain what he'd seen bike riding up on the Shore Highway that afternoon.

He described Damian Rose as English looking: "a tall blond Englishman."

He told the constable about the two blacks who'd come up from the beach, dripping with blood. He mentioned the expensive German rifle, the green sedan; he even described the coat from Harrods in London.

When he was finished, the black constable seemed to be smirking. He looked at Peter as if he were just another American nut on the loose. A crank case.

"Dat's good, mon," the policeman said. "Next, please," he called out the open office door.

Peter could feel himself starting to get a little angry. "Hey, could you wait a minute?" he said.

"Slow down for just a second, please. Okay? I understand that you're seeing a lot of very upset people tonight. I know it's crazy around here. . . . But what about this Englishman?"

"I took notes." The black man held up his pad. "Anyway, we already know about dem killers. Colonel Dred. Bad-ass. You know about Dred, mon? Nah, you don't know 'bout Dred."

"I don't know much about him." Peter tried to break through to the policeman. "But I saw a blond *white* man up there where those two poor kids were killed. I saw a lot of blood on a couple of black guys who looked like they'd just strangled a grammar-school class with their bare hands. I got scared, and I don't get scared very easily."

Once again the policeman seemed to be smirking. He was so know-it-all in his attitude, Peter wanted to rap him.

"I know, mon. I know it. Blond Englishmon type. Tall. Green car license starts CY. Check it out for you, mon. Check it out. . . . Okay—*who's next with stories here?*"

As the only legitimate witness walked out of the investigation . . . as the unbelievable confusion and mistakes just started to mount . . . Dr. Meral Johnson wandered out on the dark Plantation Inn grounds.

CHAPTER SEVEN

People never want to die, for some
strange reason. Especially young people.
Especially young, unfulfilled singles on
vacations they can't afford. Originally, we'd
planned the first machete murders for the
island's version of Club Mediterranee. The
Plantation Inn was chosen because of
secondary considerations.

The Rose Diary

Turtle Bay, San Dominica

In the noisy background of the Plantation Inn's
Cricket Lounge, a young, bone-tanned woman com-
plained that she would never be able to shut her
eyes and catch some sun at a beach again.

"Two murders. Just like the movies," someone
was saying—a short-haired man with a coke spoon
dangling around his neck.

Up at the lounge bar, Peter Macdonald talked to his girlfriend, Jane Cooke. He also served up gallons of planter's and boom-boom punch; rum toddies; Jamaica coffee; swizzles; fog-cutters—and an amazing quantity of good old-fashioned neat whiskey.

"I know how paranoid this sounds," he said to Jane, "but the police didn't seem to want to listen."

"That constable took your statement. He did, didn't he?"

"Yeah. I guess. But he seemed to have the whole thing wrapped up, Janie. Colonel Dred! Colonel Dred! Forget everything else. The tall blond man. The fancy rifle. Jesus, I don't know. I *hope* they're right. . . . It's just that they weren't very professional about it. It was like Ted Mack's *Original Amateur Hour* in there."

"Ahhh, Pee-ter, mon."

The lilting voice of the lounge calypso singer drifted across the room.

Then the singer whistled into his microphone. He tapped the mike with a long, effeminate fingernail. Blew softly into strange, snaky bamboo pipes.

"No need be afraid of Leon," he whispered to his white audience. Couples out of John O'Hara and John Marquand. Lots of bright WASPY green in their outfits—green and Bermuda pink.

He sang to them. "San Dominic' woman's love day say . . . is lak a mornin' dew. . . . Jus' as lakly it fall on de horse's turd . . . as on de rose."

The singer laughed. A pretty imitation of Geoffrey Holder.

A few people in the dark, red-lanterned bar started to clap.

Peter Macdonald pulled at a bicycle bell hidden somewhere in the liquor bottles over the bar.

"I wan' to sing yo peoples lubbley song 'bout sech a ooman," the singer went on. "'Bout her rose. An' . . . well, you know it, my friends . . . de unworty objet ub dat gal's affection. Me own rival. *A real shit!*"

At the same time, Chief of Police Meral Johnson walked down damp stone stairs, then along a row of cells in the dimly lit medieval basement of the Coastown jail.

Walking behind him was a lineup of seven policemen and clerks. Nearly everyone in the Coastown jail at that late hour.

The somber parade turned down another row of cells. Then another. At the end of the third row, a tall, perspiring constable waited beside an open, steel-plated door.

Inside the cell, the chief of police could already see the white man who shot Leon Rachet the previous morning.

The mysterious, middle-aged white man was lying on his cot with both arms spread wide. His hairy bare legs dangled off one end of the bed. A puddle of urine and blood ran out of the cell, right down a big drain in the dirty corridor.

While Dr. Johnson had been out at the Plantation Inn, the man had been murdered.

Killed in his bed. In jail. By a sugar-cane machete.

The crude knife was sticking out of the dead man's hairy belly—a red wool cap hung carefully on its hilt.

"Monkey Dred," Johnson whispered.

"Pee-ter! Pee-ter!"

The calypso singer's sweet voice drifted across the Cricket Lounge.

"Tell me dis one ting, mon? . . . What be de difference be-tween Irishmon wedding an' Irishmon wake?"

Sulking, a little embarrassed, Peter resisted. He didn't want to be a part of the show tonight. Not tonight. Not with the image of the mutilated nineteen-year-olds crawling through his mind like bloodworms.

"So what's the difference?" someone called out from the dark bar.

Peter looked at Jane and could see the same— what? distaste? nausea?

"One less drunk?" The chestnut-haired man finally gave in; yanked the asinine bicycle bell, felt— very strangely, dumbly—a little homesick.

May 3, 1979, Thursday
Tourists
Flee
Resort
Hotels!

Nine murders were reported around the resort island on the third day.

Two knifings; two pistol shootings; a forced drowning; four machete killings.

Sophisticated TV news crews began to arrive on San Dominica in the early afternoon: hippie cameramen, soundmen who looked like NASA engineers, "California Dreaming" directors, assistant directors, reporters, and commentators. Crews came from ABC, CBS, NBC. They came from local stations in New York City, Miami, and Chicago. Apparently the machete murders were an especially popular item in Chicago and New York.

Reporters and crew members were given hazard-

ous-duty pay just as they received for covering combat assignments, urban riots, or madmen on the loose.

Newspaper correspondents—quieter types, less Los Angelese—started to arrive, too.

They came from the States, of course, but they also began to come in from Western Europe; from Africa and Asia; and especially from South America. The Third World countries were particularly well represented.

The newshounds smelled a revolution!

Meanwhile, police and army experts were predicting that the sudden, mind-boggling violence would either die down completely—or flare up all over the Caribbean.

So far—even with Colonel Dred as an obvious target—it was a hell of a mystery.

CHAPTER EIGHT

We had learned long before we ever saw
the Caribbean that beautiful scenery
provides the most chilling background for
any kind of terrorism.

The Rose Diary

May 3, 1979; Titchfield Cove, San Dominica

Thursday Morning. The Third Day of the Season.

Dressed in loose-fitting blue jeans and a blue cotton T-shirt, Damian Rose climbed hard and as fast as possible. He moved toward huge outcroppings of black rock poised above the Shore Highway.

High up in the rocks, the lazy island trade winds had chiseled two primitive heads over centuries and centuries—neither of which, Rose was thinking as he moved along, had been worth the hot air and bother.

His fingers curled into small cracks, Rose pulled himself up over countless tiny ledges toward the sea blue sky. He could feel his boots crunching loose rocks as he ascended; he could taste his own salty sweat.

After fifteen minutes of hard climbing, he pulled himself onto a barren ledge of flat rock. The small jut of rock was about four feet long, less than three feet wide. Close up, the black rock was loaded with specks of shiny mica. Mica and tiny seagull bones.

From the gull's high burial ground, Damian could see everything he needed to see.

The morning after the Turtle Bay murders had turned out crisp and pure, with a high blue sky all over the Caribbean. A hawk flew directly over his head, watching the empty highway and watching him, it seemed.

Far below, the sea was choppy in spite of the pacific blue skies. Brown reefs were visible on the outskirts of Titchfield Cove.

There was a long, dramatic stretch of crystal beach that ended in another hill of high black rocks.

Damian Rose began to concentrate on a slightly balding dark-haired man and his two children as they walked down the perfect beach.

The three of them were getting their feet and legs wet in the creamy surf . . . walking along as if they were waiting for the man who photographed such moments for postcards and greeting cards.

Damian took out two lengths of streamlined black pipe. He began to screw them together. Made a barrel. Screwed the longer pipe into a lightweight stock. Made a gun. Added a sniper's scope from his backpack.

The dark-haired man, Walter Marks, dived over a small blue wave and disappeared.

His boy and little girl seemed leery of the water. Attractive children, Rose bothered to notice. Two blonds, like their mother.

Their father was an ass to take them out the morning after the machete killings. A shallow, foolish ass. Promised them a vacation. Always kept his promises.

Rose put the sight of the German rifle to his eye. Thin crosshairs that didn't meet.

He watched Marks's slick brown hair surface in bubbles. The man stood up, and the water was only to his waist. He had a very hairy chest: brown hair that seemed to turn black in wet tufts.

Through the powerful Zeiss sight, Walter Marks seemed close enough to reach out and touch.

Rose saw the Cuban waving from high weeds not far behind the beach. "Shooting goldfish in a bowl": he remembered a strange, wonderful saying.

Damian squeezed off just one shot.

Walter Marks fell over backward in the three-foot-high water. He looked as if he were trying to step back over a wave to amuse his children.

The bullet had gone through the center of his forehead, spitting out brain like a corkscrew.

The children began to scream at once. They hugged each other and seemed to be dancing in the suddenly pinkish water.

Kingfish and the Cuban appeared with the machete. The Roses' inspired buck-and-wing team. Wading out into the sea.

Fortunately, but at the same time unfortunately for the Marks children, there had to be witnesses this time. The witnesses were to be the children themselves.

Too bad, Rose thought for a split second. And yet perfect.

The cold-blooded murder of the president of ASTA. The public execution of the president of the American Society of Travel Agents.

Who deserved it for being such a pompous fool. For ignoring all the warnings.

Turtle Bay, San Dominica

Somewhere in the U.S. Marine annals, it says that "a Marine on Embassy Duty is an Ambassador in uniform."

Clearly out of uniform—dressed in gray insignia

shorts and nothing else—twenty-four embassy duty marines spent the morning of May 3 conducting a dreaded sector search of the beach at Turtle Bay.

The muscular soldiers picked up driftwood, sea-horses, periwinkle, clear, rubbery jellyfish. They picked up chewing gum, matches, lint, stomach-turning shreds of human flesh, strands of hair, the nub of a woman's finger. They picked up everything on the beach that wasn't sand: literally everything.

They put whatever they found into heavy-duty plastic bags marked XYXYXY.

Then the marine captain ordered his men to "rake the sand back to normal."

Hand in hand up on the Shore Highway, Peter Macdonald and Jane Cooke watched the dubious detective work going on all over the beach.

Beside a big man like Macdonald, Jane seemed slighter than she really was. Close up, she was somewhat big-boned—an old-fashioned midwestern beauty right out of Nelson Algren. Freckles, dimples, long blond hair a river of curls.

Before she'd become a social director at the Plantation Inn, Jane had been a high-school English teacher in Pierre, South Dakota. At twenty-one she'd married another English teacher; miscarried their future Joyce Carol Oates in a Pierre shopping mall; was separated at twenty-three.

After that, Jane had decided to see a little bit more of the world than the Dakota Badlands. She'd traveled down to South America. Traveled up to the Caribbean. Haiti, finally San Dominica. Then Peter Macdonald. Crazy, funny Peter—who reminded her of a poem—also of a Simon & Garfunkel song called "Richard Cory."

Before he'd come to the Plantation Inn, Peter had been, first and foremost, the last and least worthy (in his own mind, anyway) of the six Macdonald brothers. Three college baseball stars, two academic big deals—and then Peter. Little Mac.

As a result, Peter had become a cadet at the U.S. Military Academy at West Point (like his father—Big Mac). He'd left West Point after his second class year—become a soldier for real. A Special Forces sergeant; decorated twice; shot in the back once. A war hero—whatever that was in the mid-seventies.

With a little luck and good planning that winter, he'd wound up in the sunny Caribbean. R&R . . . "Getting your shit together," his suddenly contemporary-as-hell father had written in a long letter. . . . He'd met Jane in September, and they'd moved in together by the end of the month. Both of them living and working at the ritzy Plantation Inn . . . not bad.

Jane had only one question about the marines working down on Turtle Bay. "What in heck do they do it for?"

Peter found himself smiling. "Rake dirt? . . . I

don't know what for. *They* don't know. *Somebody* probably knew why at one time or another. Now they just do it. Soldiers rake dirt on every military base in the world."

"Well, it's the dumbest thing I've ever seen. One of the dumbest. It's dumber than baseball." Jane grinned.

"It's a whole lot dumber when you're behind the rake. That's okay, though. . . . Let's walk. . . . By the way, baseball isn't dumb."

They walked up through a lot of banana and breadfruit trees. A pretty jungle with a few parrots and cockatoos to spice things up. Kling-kling birds, too.

Macdonald took his baseball cap out of a back pocket and tugged it on to keep out bugs.

"What are you going to do now, Peter?" she finally asked him.

Macdonald sighed. "I don't know what I should do. . . . Maybe the murders were just what the police say. Dassie Dred making sure his people get fair trials from now on. No more hanging sentences. Simple as that."

"And the Englishman?"

"Ah, the bloody white man. The damn, tall, blond, *Day-of- the*-fucking-*Jackal* character. Complicating our beautifully uncomplicated existence."

Peter picked up a rock and sidearmed a high inside curve around a banana tree. "You know what else? . . . I'm starting to feel bad about wasting my life all of a sudden. . . . Anything but that, dear God. Please don't make me feel guilty about feeling good. See, I was just in this fucked-up war and . . ."

Jane put her arms around Peter's slim waist. Behind him she could see sharp blue sea through palm leaves. It was all so perfect that most of the time she didn't completely believe in it.

"Tell me this, Peter Macdonald. Where does it say that *not killing yourself working* is wasting your life?"

Macdonald smiled at the wise blond girl. He held on to one of her soft breasts and kissed her mouth gently. "I'm not sure . . . but it's engraved on my brain. I feel that exact thought grinding away in there every day that I'm down here. Every time I dive into the deep blue sea."

He put his hand over his mouth. When he did that, his voice came out deep and strange. *"Get yourself a decent job, Macdonald, you bum. Shape up before it's all over, Pete. Be somebody or be gone. . . . Anyway"*—his voice came back to normal—"I guess I have to do something about the Englishman, huh, Laurel?"

Jane winced slightly. In their little South Seas fantasy world—their paradise life in the Caribbean—she was called Laurel; Peter was Hardy-ha-ha.

"I wish you wouldn't," the blond woman said. "Really. I'm serious, Peter."

"I have to try one more thing," Peter said.

For that moment, though—at 8:30 on Thursday morning—the two of them made a little clearing on the pretty hillside. They lay down together like two missionary lovers.

Peter pulled gently at the white shirt knotted under her breasts. Jane lifted her slender arms. Let the loose white shirt go up around her neck, shoulders.

"I love you so much," she whispered. "Just thought I'd say that."

He took a soft, cool breast in each hand. Unzipped her shorts. Slid shorts and panties down over her dark brown legs.

She unbuckled red L. L. Bean suspenders, pulled at blue jeans, helped him out of underwear and baseball hat. He was kissing her everywhere, tonguing her nipples for a long, lazy time. Feeling soft, invisible down on her stomach. Smelling coconut oil.

Peter entered Jane slowly, an inch at a time, then long, slow thrusts. . . .

They stopped each other twice. Delaying, saving. Then they came with little spasms that made them dizzy. A long climax, both of them whispering as if they were in church.

When they finally sat up again, all the marines

were gone. Turtle Bay looked perfect and innocent again. Raked neat as a farmer's field.

Chuk, chuk, chuk was the sound machetes made cutting sugar cane.

Chik, chik, chik was the sound Peter heard.

Chik, chik, chik.

Chik, chik, chik.

Chik, chik, chik. Cashoo.

Peter had found Maximilian Westerhuis tabulating fancy yellow-on-white hotel bills in his eight-by-eight office, wearing steel-rimmed eyeglasses, looking somewhat mathematical. A cipher.

The coal black machine the German used for counting looked as if it had somehow survived the Weimar Republic. In addition to the machine, there were red-and-blue-edged letter envelopes scattered all over the inn manager's desk: news from the Fatherland.

Resting on some of the papers was a big foamy mug of Würzburger dark.

Peter stood in the doorway, reluctant to announce himself to the huffy young German. Then the pecking on the adding machine stopped.

"Peter, what do you want? Can't you see I'm too busy with all of these fools checking out of the hotel?"

Looking slightly dizzy, the white-blond man eyed him with distaste over his wire rims. "Macdonald, *what is it you want*!'' The strident voice came once again.

I want to beam myself right back out of your office, Peter was thinking. You're so full of yourself, hot shit and vinegar, that it turns my stomach.

''I have to ask a personal favor,'' Peter said softly, wincing inside at the toady way the words came out. Playing Heinrich Himmler to Max's Hitler. ''I need to borrow your BMW.''

The inn manager huffed out a small nose laugh. ''Borrow my motorcycle? Have you gone mad? Leave me alone. Get out of here.''

''Yeah, well, in a minute. . . . You see, I've got to talk to somebody else about the man I saw on the Shore Highway yesterday. It's bothering me, Max. I've got to find out why the hell they—''

''You talked to *me*, Macdonald,'' Westerhuis cut in. ''*I* talked to the stupid newspaper people. *You* talked to the policeman last night. People know about your man up on the hill, *nicht wahr*? Now I tell you, *leave*. You don't ever call me Max, by the way.''

Peter suddenly cut off all pretense of diplomacy. ''I want to talk to the American ambassador in Coastown! . . . Lives could be at issue here, Westerhuis. I need your fucking BMW for two or three hours. That's it, you know. Be a human being, huh? Pretend.''

The inn manager began to use one side of his

metal office desk like a brass drum. "Absolutely not!" he pounded. "I thought it over for five seconds, and the answer is *no*! Now get out of here. One more word and I fire you as bartender Johnny on the spot."

Peter turned away and started out of the claustrophobic office. "Peter on the spot," he mumbled. "Screw you, you Nazi love child."

"What is that I hear?" Westerhuis called out the door after him.

Then, *chik*, *chik*, *chik*, he was operating the antique tabulator again, thinking: Poor damn fool Peter Macdonald. Poor fool bartender. Should have stayed in the army for your entire life.

Outside, an expensive-looking silver key was turning the ignition of the shiny black BMW motorcycle—Peter Macdonald and Jane Cooke had taken big steps in the wrong crazy direction. Both of them were about to jump in way over their heads.

Peter said, "Sure. Max said it was okay. . . . Hang on tight, here we go!"

Which was, perhaps, the understatement of the decade.

Chapter Nine

I believed that Damian could be happy in
Europe on $10 a day. I could be content, I
think, on Jacqueline Onassis's $10,000 a
week. Sometimes I find myself reading
Cosmopolitan and identifying with Jackie.
Weird fantasy life! I've even plotted out
how I could get to marry one (or more) of
the world's richest men. . . . Damian could
be wealthy if he cared primarily about
money. Damian could be an international
film star like Bronson or Clint Eastwood.
Or the still-life president of General
Motors. Damian could be, Damian could
be . . . sitting on rocks in Crete. Starting to
repeat myself as I approach thirty. Scary
thoughts for your basic hick out of
Nebraska.

The Rose Diary

Coastown, San Dominica

In the middle of a world of hack-arounds—fruit and straw vendors, fruits, package-rate tourists, cabdrivers by the gross, beeping double-decker buses—Carrie Rose looked around Politician Square and tried to single out one poor bugger who had to be sacrificed that morning.

She concentrated on ten or so long-haired dopers grazing near the entrance to Wahoo Public Beach.

Here pure white trash floated down from the United States . . . semiacceptable bums in tie-dyed *REGGAE* T-shirts. In *LOVE RASTAFARI* T-shirts. Drinking out of Blue Label beer cans. Chewing gum to a man. Eating fresh coconut.

Beyond choosing the comatose group, it was all too disturbingly arbitrary, Carrie couldn't help thinking. Depressing. Damian's sort of game.

Finally she settled on a short, skinny one. A freak's freak among the idle young Americans. Carrie named him the Loner.

The Loner appeared to be nineteen or twenty. Dirty jeans and a buckskin vest over his bare, sunken chest. Long, stringy blond hair. Wide moon eyes.

The Loner was also smoking island marijuana like a morning's first cup of Maxwell House coffee.

Carrie Rose stopped a schoolboy walking on her side of the triangular street section. A pretty brown boy of eight or nine. Books all neat and nice, held together in a red rubber sling. She asked him if he had time to earn fifty cents before his classes started that morning.

When the boy said that he did, Carrie pointed through the crowds. She directed his eyes until he saw the long-haired white man in the gold vest.

The Loner had moved up against the wall of a paint-scabbing boathouse. "Holding up the walls," they used to say back in her hometown, Lincoln, Nebraska.

"All you have to do," Carrie explained to the schoolboy, "is take this letter to that man. Give him this five dollars here. Tell him he has to deliver my letter to Fifty Bath Street. *Fifty Bath Street*. . . .

"Now tell me what you have to do for your fifty cents."

The little black boy was very serious and bright. He repeated her instructions exactly. Then the boy's face lit up.

"Hey, missus, I could deliver yo' letter myself."

Carrie's hand sunk deep into her wallet for the money. "No, no." She shook her head. "That man over there will do it. And you should tell him that a big black man is watching him. Tell him the letter is going to the black man's girlfriend."

"All right. All right. Give me everything. I take it to him all right."

The boy disappeared while crossing the square

in the hectic, colorful crowd. Carrie panicked. Started to cross the street herself.

Then the boy suddenly resurfaced near the lounging hippies. He approached the Loner, grinning a mile, waving the long yellow envelope.

The long-haired man and the boy negotiated in front of the boathouse.

A buttery sun was rising up just over the building's buckling tin roof. SAN DOMINICA—BEST PLACE IN THE WORLD was painted in red on the shack.

Finally the Loner accepted the letter.

Carrie sat on a bench and took out the morning *Gleaner*. COUPLE SLAIN ON BEACH. Cross-legged, wearing her large horn-rimmed glasses, she was among twenty or thirty tourists reading books and newspapers down a long line of sagging white benches.

The Loner looked up and down the crowded street for his benefactor. Very paranoid, apparently. Then the man did an odd little bebop step for whoever was watching. "Dyno-mite." They would find out his nickname later that day.

Finally the Loner headed off in the direction of Trenchtown District.

To deliver a soon-to-be-famous letter at 50 Bath Street.

The American embassy in Coastown was wonderfully quiet, Macdonald was thinking.

A little like West Point's Thayer Hall in the lull of summertime. Like the University of Michigan at Ann Arbor, where he'd spent one lonely, lazy summer after the army.

Green-uniformed security men walked up and down long corridors on the balls of their spongy cordovans. Whispery receptionists whispered to messengers about the latest machete murder. Friendly casuarina trees waved at everybody through rows of bay windows in the library.

Peter passed the plush wood and dark leather furniture in every room and hallway. Heavy brass ashtrays and cuspidors left over from the Teddy Roosevelt era. The smell of furniture polish was everywhere. Lemon Pledge furniture polish and fresh-cut hibiscus and oleander.

Peter decided that it was all very official and impressive—very American, in some ways—but also very cold and funereal.

And frightening.

Dressed in a neatly pressed Henry Truman sports shirt—windblown palm trees and sailboats on a powder blue background—with a permanent flush in his cheeks, Peter was led up to his hearing by a starchy butler type. A haughty black in a blue holy communion suit.

Up thick-carpeted stairways. Down deserted passageways with nicely done oil portraits of recent presidents on all the wall space. Up a winding, creaking, wooden stairway.

Finally, into the doorway of a cozy third-floor office. A neat room where some teenager could have had the bedroom of his dreams.

A young man, a public safety adviser, was sitting at a trendy, refinished desk inside the attic room. Very suntanned and handsome, the man struck Peter as a case study favoring the pseudoscience of reincarnation. The subconsul was an exact lookalike for the dead American actor Montgomery Clift.

"Mr. Campbell." The snippy black literally clicked his heels. "A Mr. Peter Macdonald to see you, sir."

"Hi," Peter said. "I'm sorry to bother you like this."

"No bother. Sit down. Have a seat."

Peter sat on a wine red settee across from Campbell. Then, talking with a soft midwestern accent— vaguely aware of the *Helter-Skelter* horrors and dangers he was officially associating himself with—he began to tell Brooks Campbell what he'd seen. . . .

The two black men chugging up through high bush from the beach at Turtle Bay.

The blood so bright, stop sign red, it looked as if it had to be paint.

The striking blond man forever framed among sea grapes and royal palms in his mind.

The expensive German-made rifle. The green sedan. The jacket from London . . . all of it happening roughly parallel with the place where the two nineteen-year-olds had been killed and mutilated, had their corpses desecrated beyond belief.

By the end of the strange, appalling story, a new, wonderful sensation: Peter felt that he'd actually been listened to.

Campbell was leaning way back on his swivel chair, smoking a True Blue cigarette down to the filter, looking very serious and interested. Looking like a young, troubled senator in his starchy blue shirt with the rolled-up sleeves.

"You said you'd gone around another bend in the Shore Highway." Campbell spoke in a deep orator's voice. A hint of wealth in it; a slight lockjaw tendency. "Did you see the black men actually join up with this other man? The blond man?"

That was a good point, Peter considered. Not a bad start. He had never seen the men actually get together.

"No. I was really going on the bike by then. It wasn't the kind of thing you wanted to stop and . . . well, you know . . . the whole thing lasted about thirty seconds."

Peter began to smile. An involuntary, nervous smile. A serious moment of doubt and vulnerability. He caught himself twisting his sports shirt between his thumb and forefinger.

Campbell sat forward on his swivel chair. He

crushed out his cigarette. "I've got to ask you to take my word about something, Peter." He leveled Macdonald with a stare.

"I'll try. Shoot."

"Turtle Bay *was* an isolated incident. It was retribution for a harsh Supreme Court decision here in Coastown. . . . Except for the fact that some Americans were killed, it's a local affair. I don't know if you've read anything about the murders at Fountain Valley golf course on St. Croix—"

"Okay. That theory is all well and good," Peter broke in. "But what about this blond monkey? Seriously. Can you tell me what a white man was doing there with a sniper's rifle? Kind of gun you use to blow John Kennedy's Adam's apple out with. Tell me something comforting about that guy and I'll go home happy. Won't bother you ever again."

Brooks Campbell got up from his desk. He made a tiny crack in the drapes, and bright sunlight pierced into the attic room. "You know what, Peter?" he said, giving just a hint of a slick politician's smile. "I *don't know* what in hell a white man was doing up there.

"Let me tell you a little state secret, though. I've listened to over, oh, fifty people who have *clues* about Turtle Bay. I've listened to the police, the army . . . and *everything* I've heard so far points to Colonel Dassie Dred. I don't know what else to tell you here, Peter."

Campbell stopped his pacing. His mind had been wandering back to a meeting one year ago in the Nevada desert. To slick projections made about Damian and Carrie Rose.

Christ! They'd screwed up already. Rose was blown wide open. The great mysterious Damian Rose—whom even they had never been able to see.

Campbell looked across the small attic room at Peter Macdonald. His eyes fell to the Hawaiian shirt. "Trust me, Peter." He smiled halfheartedly, his mind still on the Roses. "Leave my secretary a number where I can reach you."

Peter didn't answer right away. Mind going a little crazy on him. In God we trust. All others pay cash, Brooks. . . . He had the sudden nauseating feeling that he was all by himself again.

"Jesus," slipped out of his mouth.

Then the surly black secretary came back, and the interview was over.

Peter left the big white mansion in a sweat. He couldn't remember feeling so alone and down in a long, long time. Not since the march into Cambodia.

As he walked through the pretty embassy grounds, he nodded at the well-scrubbed marines on guard duty, smiled at the Walt Disney World tourists—but he kept thinking back to the government actor Brooks Campbell.

Who, meanwhile, stood behind a big dormer window up on the third floor. Smoking a cigarette, watching Macdonald go out the front gates.

The Witness.

Just before noon the Loner shuffled down Bath Street in Coastown.

The long-haired man, "Dyno-mite," was holding Carrie Rose's letter as if it were a birthday party invitation his mother had told him to keep nice and clean.

Chachalacas and a cockatoo chatted up and down the pretty, quiet side street. A few pariah dogs barked at him, and the Loner barked back. Some goats were lunching mindlessly on garbage and scruffy back lawns—and the Loner remembered that he was hungry, too.

And stoned out of his mind. Wasted. Blown away. Feeling rather nice on the balmy afternoon.

Fifty Bath turned out to be the office of the *Evening Star* newspaper.

The Loner rang a bell hanging loose by its own electrical wires. Then he waited.

In a few minutes a black girl with hibiscus in her hair appeared in the doorway. The girl was laughing as if she'd just been told a joke. She accepted the manila envelope. Then suddenly, unbelievably, loud shotgun blasts shattered the quiet of the side street.

The Loner was thrown hard against the doorjamb

and wall. His skinny, needle-tracked arms flew up, palms out flat. His hair flew like a dirty mop being shaken out. Bullets held him against the wall, stitching his chest and face. He was dead before he slid to the ground.

A few minutes later the *Evening Star*'s flabbergasted black editor was trying to read the letter the man had brought. The letter appeared to be from Colonel Dassie Dred—Monkey Dred.

It promised the most severe and unusual punishments if the white foreigners didn't leave San Dominica.

It promised that if the letter itself wasn't printed for all to see in the evening news, a similar delivery would be made at 50 Bath Street the following morning.

At 12:30 Dr. Meral Johnson arrived at the tiny newspaper office. The black police chief examined the gaping hole in the newspaper office's front door. He looked at the dead man. Talked with the young girl who had accepted the letter. Sent his men to scour the neighborhood, to try to find out if anyone had witnessed the shooting.

Then it was Meral Johnson himself who came up with the name "Dead Letter" to describe the delivery. Thus far, Dr. Johnson realized sadly, it was just about his only contribution to the extraordinary case.

CHAPTER TEN

The crème de la crème of the Intelligence
people are the plodding bureaucrats. The
worst of them are the Ivy League and Eton
boys. And in this case, the crème didn't
necessarily rise to the top.

The Rose Diary

Fairfax Station, Virginia

That afternoon and evening, Washington, D.C.,
was filled with ironic talk about the failure of Vietnamese and Chinese negotiators to agree on a peace
settlement. Speechwriters for Jimmy Carter were
already busy preparing a vow that America would
keep its pledge abroad; that America would not turn
back to isolationism.

Thirteen miles southwest of the capital was Harold Hill's Old Virginny Home on six neat acres in

Fairfax Station. The land was closed in by green rolling hills and white picket fences. It was rich in honeysuckle, boxwoods, dogwoods, and full-bred domestic animals. On one of the white fence gates was the hand-painted sign OUR OLD VIRGINNY HOME.

Perhaps! But when Harold Hill was away from home, he sometimes referred to the place as "Vanilla Wafer."

From every vantage point, the Hill homestead seemed innocent and indistinctly sweet. The most secretive thing anyone might even associate with the normal-looking place was the presence of one of A. C. Nielsen's famous survey TVs.

But never murder, or mayhem, or Intelligence.

Which is more or less the way Harry the Hack wanted it.

On most weekday evenings during the spring and early summer, Hill was in the habit of playing hardball with his son, Mark. Mark was fourteen, a budding star in Babe Ruth league baseball. Every night that there was no game, Mark had to throw his father one hundred strikes or be damned.

Hill was haunched awkwardly over loose-fitting Top-Siders that night; just sweating nicely; starting to enjoy the exercise—the warm itch in his palm under a Rawlings catcher's mitt.

Suddenly he was called to the house by his wife, Carole. "Long distance calling," she shouted from the porch in an Alabama accent she hadn't lost while living in eight different countries. "It's Brooksie Campbell."

Hill excused himself to his son, then jogged up toward the big Colonial-style house. On the way inside, forty-four-year-old Harold Hill started to feel a little turmoil in his stomach.

Brooks Campbell just didn't call you at home. Not to shoot the bull, anyway. There was something about this terrorism bullshit—Campbell's so-called specialty—that didn't sit well with Harold Hill.

Terrorism was something for the Arabs and Israelis. The Irish. The Symbionese Liberation Army. Something for the little people who *had* to play dirty. Terrorism just wasn't something Americans should be getting involved with.

Inside his den, Hill dialed an eight hundred number on a phone he kept in a locked desk drawer.

What would happen—he continued his thought from outside—if a major power started playing dirty pool on a regular basis? All-out, no-holds-barred dirty? What would happen if America found a real "guerrilla" war? Shee-it! is what would happen. A return to the Dark Ages.

Hill punched an extension button, and the call from the Caribbean was switched onto a safe line, a scrambler.

He could still see Mark outside. Throwing high pop-ups over an old spruce. Catching them basket style like Willie Mays. The boy had an incredible throwing arm. Incredible.

Just as he began to think that the telephone switch-over was taking too long, he heard Brooks Campbell's voice.

"Hello, Harry." A slightly muffled Campbell— his deep stage voice sounded a little muddy. "The reason I'm calling, Harry—"

Harold Hill let out a short, snorting laugh meant to slow down the younger man. "I think I'm going to sit down for that. For the reason you're calling."

"Yeah, sit down. It's not good news. . . . It turns out, uh, that Rose was seen by a man at Turtle Bay yesterday. How about that? We buy someone *even we haven't seen*, a fucking genius, supposedly, and he's immediately made by somebody else. Shit, Harry, if I didn't know better, I'd say that somebody is fucking around with us. At any rate, I don't want to take any chances with this."

"Does Rose know he was seen? Tell me the whole thing, Brooks."

"Basically, he knows his situation," Campbell said. "He called us today. At least his wife did. She said they want to take care of it themselves. Cute?"

"Terrific."

"The man who saw him is a nobody, thank God. American, though. . . . By the way, Rose shot and cut up the president of ASTA this morning. Harry, they're freelancing like crazy now. I don't even remember the original plan we were shown. He skipped a meeting with me last night. They've gone fucking nuts on us."

Harold Hill closed his eyes and visualized Campbell. Brooks Corbett Campbell. Princeton man. WASP from New London, Connecticut. Slated for big things at the Agency. Neo-Nazi, in Hill's humble opinion. Kind of guy who always thinks he knows what's best for everybody else.

"Well, uhhh . . . I think we have to go along with them a while longer. Don't you? Maybe *you* ought to lay hands on this witness. It seems to me that we may need him to identify Rose. Eventually, anyway. . . . I have no intention of letting them leave the island after this is over. That's an obvious stroke."

"Sounds good." Brooks Campbell raised his voice above some transatlantic chatter. "That's pretty much the way I see it right now."

Hill paused for a moment. He thought he ought to try to cheer Campbell up a bit. S.O.P.

"All right. Okay on that," said Harry the Hack. "Now let me have the bad news."

Young Brooks Campbell tried to laugh. Your basic combat camaraderie. "Thought you'd never ask," he said.

Coastown, San Dominica

"Let's try to look at this shitty mess logically," Jane suggested.

Peter didn't answer. He was way off someplace else. At the artillery range outside Camp Grayling in central Michigan. Shooting tin cans off Brooks Campbell's head. With a bazooka.

At ten that night the two of them were out on the dark patio of Le Hut Restaurant, trying to comprehend mass murder. Occasionally picking through a stew pot of oily bouillabaisse. Both of them about as hungry as the shrimp in the pot.

Peter finally raised his puppy-dog brown eyes to her and shrugged. "Who could come up with that kind of idea? . . . Slicing up two nineteen-year-old kids like Jack the Ripper?"

Jane sat with her chin in the palms of thin hands. Serious, she looked like an older version of Caroline Kennedy. She was catching the eye of all the black waiters.

"Probably the same kind of creep who would make two little kids watch their own father die," she answered. "It just makes me feel so awful. Creepy and sick. Really shitty—besides being scared."

Thinking back on the scene at the American embassy, Peter began to feel a little useless, motelike. Little Mac fucks it up again. . . . Maybe he just hadn't explained himself well enough, he thought. *Something* sure had gone wrong at the embassy. Because the tall blond man *was* important one way or the other. He had to be.

Jane pointed out to the street. Playful grin on her face; premachete smile. "I didn't know one of your brothers was down on the island. Heh, heh."

Right in front of Le Hut a street clown was entertaining a small crowd. The scruffy clown was white. BASIL: A CHILDREN'S MINSTREL said his hand-painted sign.

Basil was a young man behind all his Indian and clown paints. Around the eyes he seemed very serious about the show, even a little sad. Only dressed the way he was—raggy canary-yellow pantaloons, an outrageous pastel nightcap—the man also seemed pixilated.

"Love is the answer," he said to natives and a few tourists walking past him on Front Street. "Love is the answer," he whispered to the people eating and drinking in Le Hut.

"Ahhh," Jane whispered to Peter, winked, talked like Charlie Chan. "But what is question?" She saw that he was still partially lost in his own thoughts. Turtle Bay. What had upset him at the U.S. embassy?

"Do you know any children's tricks? Children's minstrel tricks?" she whispered across the table. "Macduff? Are you there? Are you here with me?

Or are you Sherlock Holmes off solving great murders?''

Peter smiled and blushed. ''Sorry. I'm here. Hello!''

He traveled back to the cafe from faraway places: Vietnam; his parents' house up on Lake Michigan, where every summer for six straight years Betsy Macdonald came and dropped another brown-haired, brown-eyed baby boy. The Super Six.

''Children's tricks?'' Peter grinned. Had a rush of feeling for this eccentric plains girl from Dakota.

He thought for just a second. Remembered something his brother Tommy used to do for his kids.

Peter picked up his Le Hut paper napkin. Twisted it tight and held it under his nose. The napkin looked like a droopy mustache. Greasy. Full of fish scraps. ''You must pay the rent,'' Peter said in an obvious villain's voice.

He switched the napkin to the side of his hair. It became a girl's ribbon. ''I can't pay the rent,'' he said in the falsetto of a heroine in distress.

Mustache voice: ''You must pay the rent!''

Ribbon voice: ''I can't pay the rent!''

He switched the napkin under his chin, where it became a puffy bow tie. Peter spoke in a voice like Dudley Do-Right. ''*I'll* pay the rent!''

Ribbon voice: ''My hero.''

Mustache voice: ''Curses, foiled again.''

''I wish it was that easy,'' Jane said.

She kissed his paper mustache. Laurel and Hardy—ha-ha. Neither of them quite full-fledged adults yet. Not in all ways. Lots of good intentions to grow up, though.

That night they slept together for the last time. Ever.

Crafton's Pond, San Dominica

Meanwhile, the first meeting between the Roses and Colonel Monkey Dred was close to its very shaky start.

Motors off, four cars sat on opposite sides of a flat, narrow field near Nate Crafton's rat-infested pond in the West Hills District. The field's regular use was for prop planes coming from, and going to, New Orleans with shipments of ganja and cocaine.

This particular night it was misty up around the pond itself. The wet grass was full of long, husky water rats.

By mutual agreement each side had brought only two cars. There were to be no more than two passengers in either auto. Since there seemed to be no way to prevent them, guns had been permitted.

Shortly before starting time, a *third* vehicle appeared on the horizon on Dred's side of the field. At 1:00 A.M.

The first violation of the treaty for this evening.

As Monkey Dred was driven forward in a noisy, British-made van, the twenty-seven-year-old Jamaican- and Cuban-trained revolutionary saw that the secret airfield was dark, without motion. Quite pretty, with a pale quarter moon set over the surrounding jungle.

The van stopped with a jolt at the edge of the field. Dred's driver flashed his headlights on and off. On and off.

Across the moonlit darkness, another set of car lights switched on, then off. Rose.

Watching the scene through a cloudy, bug-smeared windshield, Dred started to nod and smile. Rose was already accepting compromises: the *third* car. "Goan to be easy, mon," he said to his driver.

Two of the five cars then drove halfway out onto the landing field. Once again, the agreed-upon procedure. The Roses were very keen on orderly procedures, Dred was beginning to notice. Like the British in the American Revolution.

Before his van had fully stopped, the colonel jumped out and stood at rigid attention in the tall grass. Less than forty yards away, he could see Rose climbing out of some kind of American pleasure car.

The white man wasn't as big as Dred had expected. Not bigger than life, certainly. . . . He was wearing a light-colored suit with a big Panama-style hat. Very flashy. Absurdly so.

On signal, the headlights of both vehicles were

turned off. Then the two started to walk toward each other in the dark. In less than thirty seconds they were only a few feet apart. The smell of some kind of fertilizer met that of a strong French cologne.

"Yo' hab dose guns for me?" The revolutionary spoke with a heavy island patois.

Carrie Rose took off the floppy yellow hat. She smiled at Colonel Dred. "You're a dead man," she said. "My husband has you in his sights on an M-21 sniper's rifle right now. The rifle has a night sighting device, so he's watching us in a pretty green light. Care to wave?"

"I don't believe dat." The black man remained calm.

Carrie put her hat back on, and a powerful rifle shot kicked up a clod of grass not three feet away from the guerrilla.

The lights on all the cars around the field shot back on again. The black man froze. Threw a hand up to keep his people in place.

"Our intentions are good." Carrie talked as if nothing at all had happened. "But we wanted you to know that you mustn't try to do anything other than what we agreed on. We agreed only *two* cars apiece. Not three. *Two*.

"If you're still interested in guns," the tall woman continued, "you'll come to the Charles

Codd estate. Tomorrow evening at ten o'clock. Similar arrangements. *Two* cars.''

"Why yo' doin it?'' the black man finally asked. He folded his arms; stood his ground.

"We want to help you take over this island,'' Carrie said to him. She shrugged. "We're being paid to do that. Come to the Codd estate tomorrow. You'll find out everything you want to know. You'll even meet Damian.''

Carrie Rose then turned away. She left the guerrilla leader a little dumbfounded. Beginning to wonder how it happened with Castro up in the Sierra Maestra mountains. Who had come to set him up with guns and bombs?

"He's just a boy,'' Carrie said to the Cuban as she got back inside the dark American car. "Isn't it funny that they would be interested in him?''

"*Solamente tres dias mas,*'' is all the Cuban said.

Just three days more.

May 4, 1979, Friday
45 U.S.
Marshals
Arrive

CHAPTER ELEVEN

We'd carefully plotted out a funhouse
maze of confusion. Confusion on all
fronts. Like a blizzard in summer, where
it's never even snowed before. . . .

 By May 4, ordinary farmers wielding
machetes in their fields stimulated heart
attacks. A black man wading in the surf—
even an unfamiliar black lifeguard—was
enough to send piggy little whites
scurrying inside their expensive straw-
roofed huts. Fishing boats that drifted too
close to shore were waved away by private
guards with rifles. No one shut their eyes
sunbathing on the beaches. . . . And
countless tourists spent their suntime in
dingy prop airline and government offices.
Pan Am, Eastern, Prin-Air, BOAC, all put
on extra flights, but even these couldn't

accommodate the exodus. . . . So far, we
were pretty much on schedule.

The Rose Diary

*The fourth day was much quieter—four island
deaths reported. All of them grisly machete murders, however.*

*Early in the morning, forty-five United States fed-
eral marshals were flown in to help keep order in
the larger cities of San Dominica. Some of these
same State Department marshals had been used
during the American Indian uprising at Wounded
Knee.*

*Eight Vietnamese-style HSL-1 helicopters came
in from Pensacola, Florida, to help with surveillance and search work.*

*Because they'd been painted with green-and-
brown combat camouflaging, the helicopters provided one of the scarier sights for the remaining
tourists. Suddenly it looked and sounded as if they
were in the middle of an undeclared war zone. Army
helicopters were continually swooping down out of
the lush green hills, as in the opening scenes in
M*A*S*H.*

*More witnesses to the machete murders were be-
ing found: "a veritable anthology of fascinating,
conflicting stories," one French newspaper would
eventually write. Five hundred eleven people ques-*

tioned so far, but no one other than Peter Macdonald claiming to have seen a white man with the raiding parties of blacks.

The chance of Macdonald's story having any effect now seemed rather small, in fact.

There were simply too many chiefs on the scene, too many chiefs prowling around the ghoulish morgues, too many hip experts who thought they understood what was going down.

CHAPTER TWELVE

What we did on San Dominica was
something like turning loose Charles
Starkweather and Caril Fugate, Speck,
Bremer, Manson, and Squeaky Fromme.
All in one place at the same time.

The Rose Diary

May 4, 1979; Coconut Bay, San Dominica

Friday Morning. The Fourth Day of the Season.

Lieutenant B. J. Singer, a 1966 Annapolis prod-
uct, sat on an undersized aluminum beach chair,
reading a book called *Supership*. His wife, Ronnie,
lay beside him with *The Other Side of Midnight*
propped up in the sand.

Neither of the Singers was a very enthusiastic
reader.

Suddenly *Supership* slipped through B.J.'s fingers.

The shiny hardcover book hit the metal arm of the beach chair, then fell broken-backed onto the sand. B.J.'s head dropped back.

"What?" Ronnie said.

"I can't stand it." Her husband sat with his eyes closed, with coconut butter glistening all over his body. "I hate this sitting around. I feel like a goddamn kid who has to have his mother come with him every time he wants to take a swim or go explore. Or do anything!"

Ronnie Singer looked up from her paperback. She closed one eye to the bright 10:00 A.M. sun. "Oh, go ahead, then." She spoke with the softest, teasing Texas accent. "You go drown yourself, honey. Get your head cut off by the Zulus. . . . See if Mom really cares. Mom doesn't care a damn."

B.J. crossed one hairless leg over the other. The big redheaded man growled at his wife.

"Ohhh . . . Mom cares," Ronnie then cooed from her beach blanket.

"I would like . . . to take off this itchy swimsuit now. On *our* own personal private beach. And soak up some of *our* own private sun on my own shriveled private parts. And dip those poor neglected bastards in *our* sparkling blue sea. . . . Just like the

TV ad suggested. Remember the TV ad for this place?"

Ronnie Singer closed her book with a dull thud. The little blond woman let out a large-size sigh. Her big breasts expanded impressively under a thin polka-dot strip of bathing suit. Mom, she called herself.

"All right, let's go for a walk, sailor."

"I'll do it." B.J. flashed a smile.

"I don't know if I'm brave enough to take off my clothes, though."

"Swish, swish, swish," B.J. kidded her.

"Very funny, B.J. Cool it."

They walked north through two pretty coves. To a smaller, more private beach where the big brown hulk of a wrecked schooner sat out a few hundred yards from shore.

When they came up, even-steven with the rigless boat, B.J., then Ronnie, waded out into clear blue-green water full of tiny angelfish.

Ronnie slipped off the top of her suit and let her sand white breasts float free on the water. She started to laugh, to blush even.

Once the cool water got up around his chest, the navy man turned to check out the kelly green of West Hills. "Prettiest damn jungle . . . ," he started to say.

Then he saw two shirtless blacks lying in a grove

of baby palms. Unbelievable, heart-freezing sight. You never believe it can happen to you.

"Oh, Jesus, my God," he whispered to Ronnie. "They're on this beach."

The young couple began to swim out toward the shipwreck. Slow wading at first, then an athletic breaststroke.

"Go behind it." B.J. had taken command. "You make it okay, Ronnie?"

Damian Rose's first rifle shot hit with a *thunk* eight yards in front of them.

The Singers pulled up short. Then they kept going toward the old wreck. Much more frantic now. Hard, splashing strokes.

A second shot kicked up water less than a foot away from B.J. A third shot echoed in the distance but never seemed to hit anywhere. B.J. didn't let on that he'd been hit in the back.

Finally they were in the long, cool shadow cast by the schooner. The boat towered thirty to forty feet over their bobbing heads. Ugly rot and barnacles were visible all over the sides.

As they swam around one corner of the schooner, Ronnie felt a strong sweep of water at her side. Like a cold spring. The topless woman turned her head slightly—saw a four-, maybe five-foot silverish shadow not twelve inches away. For a moment she stopped swimming altogether. Her head dipped underwater. She had quick, panicky thoughts of her two young sons back in Newport News; of her mother; of drowning.

Another silver streak surfaced at B.J.'s side. Flashing. Twisting. At least a sixty-pound great barracuda. Two of them now.

"Swim easy," B.J. gasped. "Stay behind the boat. No matter what. Swim easy, babe."

The cigar-shaped fish seemed to glide in the water. Back and forth with the larger humans; touching their tails as if exploring; showing off sharp, pointy teeth.

Feeling the pain in his upper back, B.J. finally floated under the schooner's sagging bowsprit. From there he could see the beach clearly.

He spotted the two barebacked blacks retreating up into the hills. He couldn't see the rifleman anywhere. . . . He watched the blacks until they disappeared into thick, thick jungle. Watched until the pain in his back was too great.

Then he and Ronnie paddled around the boat—a man and a woman—and the two big, surging fish.

The Singers were careful not to make sudden movements as they swam. They were careful to do as little splashing as possible. As little breathing.

And finally, when the young man and woman got into four or five feet of water—when they could just touch bottom—the great barracudas turned away. The fish flashed their tails and headed back toward the old wreck. . . . B.J. and Ronnie ran the last fifty yards to shore.

As the Singers lay on the wet sand like shipwrecked survivors, Damian Rose squeezed, squeezed, shot them both dead anyway.

CHAPTER THIRTEEN

> To be simplistic about things, I just didn't
> want to live and die in some godforsaken
> whistle-stop. Like Madame Bovary.
>
> The Rose Diary

Coastown, San Dominica

At eleven o'clock that morning, Carrie Rose lounged beside a 2,500,000-gallon saltwater swimming pool at the Coastown Princess Hotel.

Next to her at the poolside bar, a thirty-three-year-old stockbroker from New York, Philip Becker, was lamenting the decline and fall of the good life. He was also trying to put the make on Carrie.

"It is a sad, shitty affair." Philip Becker eulogized San Dominica in a most-good-natured way. "Here you finally *make time* for a vacation. You pay out two thousand, say, for ten glorious days of *not* having to schlepp around Manhattan with all the gum snappers, panhandlers, the general roll call of sewer snipes. . . . And then suddenly, slam-bam, you don't just get a little rain to ruin your good time. . . . You don't get a sunburn. . . . You get a bloody revolution!''

Carrie shook out her long sandy hair, exposed the tiniest mother-of-pearl earrings. She was beginning to smile at the way Becker was telling his dimwitted stories.

''I like the way you say that.'' She rested her hand on the back of his. ''You get a revolution!'' she repeated his thought.

''That is exactly what we have here,'' the stockbroker said. ''Machete knife behind every palm tree.'' He was beginning to stare openly at her breasts now; her long legs; brown swimmer's stomach; her crotch.

''This Dred—excuse me, *Colonel* Dred—is going to do some major league bloodletting now. Which means I'm going back to the *safer* confines of New York.''

''All of a sudden a hundred and fifty thousand tourists and landowners want to get off this island at the same time,'' Carrie said.

Philip Becker smiled. He raised his glass in a mock salute. ''To, uh . . . Colonel Monkey Dred, who, uh, ruined our respective vacations. Up yours, Monkey.''

At which point Carrie Rose decided that she liked this one well enough. Philip Lloyd Becker. A wonderfully confident man. Nearly as smooth as Damian Simpson Rose.

Smooth Philip continued to smile at her. He was gallant. Handsome. Physically nice: a walking advertisement for the New York Athletic Club. And he was as empty-headed as the proverbial dizzy blonde.

When he finally asked her if she wanted to go back to his suite, Carrie said yes.

That was the beginning of a little *cherchez la femme* side plot. Also an experiment.

Friday Afternoon

Down and out in Coastown, as disoriented as people in a Neil Simon situation, Peter and Jane first got the bum's rush at San Dominica's Government House. Then at the *Gleaner* and the *Evening Star* newspaper offices.

''If, indeed, there is a mysterious white man involved,'' a British-sounding Uncle Tom at Government House explained, ''he'll most surely turn up when we catch Colonel Dred. And, right now, we are *trying* to put all our efforts into catching Dred.''

''Well, Jesus Christ, man. Don't let us keep you

from the manhunt," Peter said before Jane could pull him away.

At noon the two of them wandered through the crowded Front Street marketplace. Children were selling green coconuts, yams, fresh fish. Tinny record-shop speakers blasted songs like "Kung Fu Fighting." Jane was getting leers and lazy smiles from all the local males.

"Take a taxi ride, lady?"

"Eat me coconut?"

One block off Front Street they went out onto the very famous and beautiful Horseshoe Beach.

"This could be the nicest day anywhere, ever," Jane said as they began to walk on the gleaming sand. "God!"

The entire surface of the Caribbean was nearly white, glittering with the brightest galaxy of stars. Jane's long blond curls were shining. . . . She was the blond beauty you always see at the beaches but nobody ever seems to get.

As the two of them walked along—in spite of their best intentions not to—they began to feel wonderfully calm and content. As if nothing really mattered except the buttery sun, getting a tan, keeping the sea spray in their faces.

"It's so grand, Peter. Kowabunga! Old Indian expression of delight and awe—from *The Howdy Doody Show*."

"Kind of makes you wonder why somebody

would pick central Michigan to settle in. Any cold climate. Oh, Caleb, isn't that the most gorgeous stretch of tundra! Let's build our house there."

"Oh . . . hush, puppy."

Walking barefoot, carrying loafers and sandals, they passed under a low wooden pier. Pilings coated with seaweed and barnacles. Some sort of hot-sauce-and-clams bar chattering overhead. As they emerged from under the dark, rotting planks, Peter happened to glance up at the boardwalk. What he saw snapped his perfect mood like a twig.

Sauntering along, carefree as tourists, were the black killers from Turtle Bay. The Cuban and King-fish Toone. Even more disturbing, the smaller of the two was pointing down at the beach. Right at Jane and him.

"Janie, we don't have time to think this out," he said, "but I want you to get ready to run like an absolute madwoman. The killers from Turtle Bay are at our beach."

Meanwhile the two blacks hurried to a set of wooden stairs twisting down to the sand. Dressed in lightweight suits and fedoras, they looked like duded-up Caribbean businessmen.

Peter looked back once and saw the two men running. Strong-looking bastards. Coming like god-damn madmen, knocking sunbathers down and stepping on them. What the hell were they figuring on? A public execution?

"Let's go. Run!"

Split-splat. Split-splat. Bare feet kicked sand high, kicking sand on people sunbathing on either side of their running track. Jane running fast, thank God. Jesus!

Trying to keep up the pace, Peter scrambled for some smart idea of what to do now. He looked back over his shoulder again. Almost trainwrecked into a family drag-assing hotel towels.

American sun dreamers doing absolutely zilch, backing away from the chase. Kitty Genovese goes to the Caribbean.

Stumbling through a particularly jammed beach towel parking lot, Jane could feel her chest and thighs starting to burn up. A slight stitch in her side. A hundred yards ahead she spotted squat limestone buildings. Showers. Dressing rooms. Shooting from the roof of the little complex, a white stairway to the boardwalk.

"Peter! Way up there!"

A few strides farther on, Peter grabbed the cabana jacket of a tall, very hairy man. "Help us!" he gasped. "Will you call the police?"

The hairy man shoved him. Stepped back. "Keep your hands off. Get away from me, you."

Nobody listened. No wonder the police and the U.S. embassy people had been so strange—they couldn't believe somebody was trying to help.

Even more terrified, the young man and woman started to run again.

They broke through crowds heading in to shower and dress in the limestone buildings. Fat boys with plastic footballs. Strong smells of sun lotions. Not really feeling these people who hit off their bodies. Numb, everything unreal.

Inside the bathhouse was a large, cool concrete room. No discernible purpose for the room. Twenty or thirty people were milling around. Rude Boys smoking corncob pipes. Four different doors going out.

"Stairs?" Peter screamed at a pink face under a big straw hat. *Princess*.

"The stairs!" Jane screamed with him now. "Tell us where!"

As *Princess* pointed left, Peter and Jane heard a commotion starting up behind them.

Suddenly a black lifeguard ran out of one of the concrete hallways. O. J. Simpson with cornbraids. He yelled in a booming voice at the two men just coming through the main entrance.

Booooomm!

A single, unbelievable explosion echoed through the bathhouse. Bright red blood sprayed all over. The shocked lifeguard crashed back into a limestone wall. He came off the wall face first, braids jangling, down onto the concrete floor.

All kinds of people were screaming, "Murder!"

in the strange bare room. People diving on the floor
. . . a hole as big as a baseball in the lifeguard's
back. Red Rorschach splatter. Total panic.

Peter and Jane were off and running again, feeling
shitty about the young black guy. Left—but they
didn't see any stairs there.

"You got any ideas?"

"No."

"Holy shit!"

Another wild mouse left and they found doors.
BATHROOM, MEN'S SHOWER, CLOSET,
WOMEN'S SHOWER, MAINTENANCE. Then
they were at a complete dead end in the building.
Fresh out of clever ideas, too.

Then Jane got her idea. "Here."

Inside WOMEN'S SHOWER, billowing steam
hit them like a sudden hot log. They saw the bare
rump of a white woman. Two rumps. Rows of gray
lockers and benches.

"Look for a place to hide in here."

The bare woman went left, Peter and Jane right.
As they did—dragging each other around sharp
locker corners—they heard the big metal door to
the corridor open and shut again.

"Nice try," Peter said.

He yanked at a wooden door and they were inside a narrow tiled room with five or six showers
running water. Down through the waterfalls they

saw a naked black woman and a little girl of about three.

The girl had a head full of creamy soapsuds. She was looking at the strange, intruding white couple as if they were the real Laurel and Hardy. The girl's mother looked terrified, though. Hands across her breasts, she started to scream.

"Please," Jane whispered, walking right back through the showers, dragging Peter. "I know how it must look, but some men are chasing us. Please don't scream."

At the end of the row of showers, the two of them slipped into a narrow alcove.

"Hidden from the front door, at least," Jane whispered to Peter.

"What do yo' want in here?" The black woman finally spoke to them.

"Please help us," Jane whispered again.

Pressed unbelievably hard against the damp tile wall, feeling her much cooler perspiration mix with the warm shower room water, she had an image that made her tremble. A clear picture of the two men coming into the shower. Firing at her and Peter. Firing at the woman. Firing at the little girl. BIZARRE SHOWER ROOM MASSACRE!

They could all hear the two men outside in the dressing rooms. Loud voices. Curses. Women screaming. Lockers slamming and opening.

"I think I'm having a nosebleed," Jane said.

Then it didn't matter. Nothing did. The two killers were inside the shower room.

Thinking about hand-to-gun combat, Peter listened to the black woman.

"What do you want in here?" she said to the two men. The same thing she'd asked him and Jane.

Neither of the Turtle Bay killers answered her. Then a man's shoes clicked down hard against the tile floor. Cleats. Coming back to check for himself. So weird not being able to see the bastard. Gun drawn?

Every muscle in Peter's and Jane's bodies began to clench. Across from them a wet mop was leaning against the wall. Weapon? . . . *Weapon*.

Peter felt unbelievably protective suddenly. Full of rage. Ready to hit the black butcher boy with the mop. Make a try for his gun. One shot at the guy in the front. Impossible odds.

Then the second man called out. Something in Spanish. *Vamonos*.

Both men left, and there was screaming outside. More doors slamming.

Jane hung up on the wall like a wet tissue. Blond hair down and dirty like a mop. Her nose bleeding.

Peter sank down to a full squatting position. Fetal position. Scared shitless position. He saw that the black woman in the shower with them was quite young. Twenty. Twenty-one. All ribs and sharp bones. The little girl was very, very pretty. Crying now because her mother was crying.

"Jesus, we're sorry," Peter said.

He and Jane waited a few minutes, made the woman promise to tell the police, then they left the dressing room.

Out in the concrete halls they didn't see either of the black killers. The building was jammed with people, though. Unbelievable shouting was blasting up and down the concrete tunnels. People were crying.

Finally they found the stairway out. They pushed and shoved their way through a wide-eyed crowd trying to find out what had happened. "*Is it another machete murder? . . .*" At the top of the stairs, Jane grabbed Peter hard around his chest. "Hold me, Peter," she said. "Just hold me for a minute."

Then, for the second straight day, the police of San Dominica took descriptions of the Cuban and Kingfish Toone.

"No blond Englishman?" the constable asked.

"He was there," Peter said. "We just didn't see him this time."

The black policeman smiled. "We didn't see him last time, either."

Las Vegas, Nevada

Friday Evening

That night in Las Vegas, the whole San Dominican operation continued toward a major blowup at breakneck speed: Great Western Air Transport reestablished contact with the Forlenza Family for the first time since Lathrop Wells.

At ten o'clock a long-haired fat man—somebody's bright idea of a professional gambler type—followed Isadore Goldman's chauffeur-driven Fleetwood out of the glittering Flamingo Hotel. Toward "downtown."

The fat intelligence man's name was Tommie Hicks, and he was a 1968 Stanford Law School graduate. Beyond that, he'd been one of the original CIA representatives at the farmhouse in Lathrop Wells.

Hicks followed Goldman two cars back down Sahara Boulevard. Into the Strip proper. Past 9:58-83 degrees on the Sahara clock. Past the Sands and three hundred other gaudy hotels.

To Caesar's Palace.

Once ensconced inside the gambling mecca, Izzie Goldman began to play high-stakes blackjack. The old man was what the croupiers call a George player: a very classy high-roller.

In his first hour at blackjack, Goldman won what

is a comfortable year's salary for most people—just over $34,000. Then the old man proceeded to lose more than $40,000, playing baccarat.

Since Tommie Hicks himself made $28,000 a year, the turnaround fascinated the hell out of him. Several times during the evening he fantasized walking up and taking away the old gangster's chips for safekeeping.

Just after 1:00 A.M. Goldman finally got up from his chair at baccarat. He headed for one of the men's rooms.

CAESAR'S it read on the swing door.

Tommie Hicks followed Goldman one swing behind. He understood perfectly well that he was no more than a centurion at this particular game.

The CIA man took the shiny urinal to the left of the old man.

Funny thing—Tommie Hicks found that he didn't have to go. Not a drop. Kind of humorous, actually. Something slightly ludicrous about sleuthing a five-foot-two, seventy-four-year-old man, anyway.

"Didn't I meet you at one of Harry Hill's parties?" he asked as the old man tinkled.

A black man—pimp—looked their way from three urinals down the line. The black stud smiled big ivory-and-gold teeth.

Izzie Goldman stared over at Hicks. He shrugged his small, rounded shoulders. "Not me, Abe."

The old gangster finished urinating and zipped

up. He walked over to the fancy sinks. Goldman pushed his gold watch up on his skinny arm and started to wash his hands.

The pimp splashed on some English Leather. Then he walked out of the bathroom without washing his hands.

"*Schvuggs* like the smell of it." Goldman nodded at the closing door. He put both hands up to his head, seemed to be stretching the neat part in his white hair. "Mr. Hill has a problem, I take it," he said, still chewing on a soggy cigar.

"Not so much Mr. Hill. There's a problem with our other two friends."

Isadore Goldman hit the *whooshing* faucets. He vaguely remembered this fat cow from the farmhouse in the desert. "A little problem, I hope."

"So far, very little . . . but we want your approval to get rid of both of them if the problem continues."

Goldman squinted at himself in the water-spotted mirror over the sink. Prune, he thought. Small prune, but prune.

He shrugged his shoulders at the younger man standing behind him. "You should know enough not to ask me. . . . But I'll tell you one thing to make your trip out here worthwhile. I would be very surprised if clever people like these Roses couldn't handle any little problems that come up."

Tommie Hicks smiled in the gilded mirror over

the old man's head. "We were very surprised," he said, "that some problems *did* come up."

Turtle Bay, San Dominica

At eight o'clock that night Macdonald stepped off a sputtering, wheezing double-decker bus heading north from Coastown. Sweat-stained alligator shirt thrown over his shoulder, he started down the neatly raked gravel driveway of the Plantation Inn.

Having persuaded Jane to stay with friends in Coastown for the night, he was all alone with the problem of being an unwanted only witness.

Apparently the local police weren't going to help. . . . The people at the U.S. embassy weren't exactly rolling out the red carpet for him, either. . . . Neither were the newspapers.

Why not? That was the $64,000 question. Why the hell not?

Plowing across the dark, deserted Plantation Inn beachfront, Peter started to wonder if all real-life crime investigations might be just as frustrating as this one. A lot of bungling around in the dark. Dumb-bunny screwups all over the place. No quick solutions. Not ever.

As he saw the outline of the beach cottage where he and Jane lived, his mind leaped back to the two black killers in Coastown. If those two were home-grown revolutionaries—Dred's people—then he was Cary Grant II.

Paranoid now—careful, anyway—he stopped walking. His heart started to pound in a way it hadn't since the day he'd left the lonely hill country of South Vietnam. From the cover of thick-leaved banana trees, he studied the silent black world like a Special Forces sergeant. . . .

Little pink honeymoon bungalow. Shadowy roof. Louvered windows. Wooden door looking as if it had been put up crooked because of the shifting sand. Dark, spooky Caribbean. Nice spot for an ambush. . . .

After watching the place for a good ten minutes, seeing no apparent trouble, nothing moving except dark palm fronds and cirrus clouds, Peter began to walk toward his home.

Halfway up the pebble-and-seashell walk, he saw a dark shape thrown across a white patio table. Moving a step closer, he recognized Max Westerhuis's Afghan, and he moaned out loud. . . . The beautiful, long-haired dog had been cut in half.

The machetes.

"Oh, Jesus God," he swore loudly. Trembled. Nearly got sick. It was the first time he'd actually seen the work of the razor-sharp knives.

The body of the thoroughbred dog—Fool's Hot Toast—had been cleanly separated across its thin rib cage. Ants and black flies were eating at the bloody crease as if it were a long, horrifying serving table.

Peter hurried past the dog and went inside. He collected clothes, money, a Colt .44 revolver hidden away in his T-shirts. His personal memento mori.

He caught his breath. Thought about where to hide. Had to decide about whom he could talk to, whom he could trust. Figure out a way to get off San Dominica altogether.

Most of all, he wanted to lead them away from Jane. Make it clear to them that their problem was with him. *The Witness.*

Wondering why they'd gone to the bother of killing the dog, wondering if they were watching him, and who the hell the tall blond man was, anyway—Peter Macdonald jogged back toward the brightly lit inn. He passed quickly through the portico—back into the dark rear parking lot. He called Jane in Coastown. Got no answer at her friend's place.

And then, at 8:45 on May 4—having damn little idea what he planned to do with it—Peter stole the hotel manager's BMW motorcycle for the second time that week.

As he slowly, quietly, rode the bike up the drive, a tall man stepped into the shadowy road now filling up with dust.

Damian Rose watched Macdonald get away—and he let him.

Peter Macdonald was right about on schedule.

Everything was.

The machetes were every bit as effective as he thought they'd be that first afternoon at Turtle Bay.

If there had been any doubt that he and Carrie were worth $1 million going into the operation, there wouldn't be after it was over. The two of them were going to be as famous as Charles Manson and Company—and marketable to boot.

May 5, 1979, Saturday
Declare
War On
Monkey
Dred

On the fifth day, San Dominican prime minister Joseph Walthey held an emotional press conference to announce that the terrible machete murders could now definitely be attributed to Colonel Dred and his very small group of dissidents.

Standing before news microphones with his wife, with the U.S. ambassador and his wife, Joseph Walthey revealed that at seven o'clock that morning a battalion of San Dominican and U.S. troops had entered the jungles of West Hills. A confrontation with Colonel Dred was expected before the end of the day.

In the meantime both Robert F. Kennedy Airport in Coastown and Kiley Airport in Port Gerry had been transformed into angry beehives of abnormal activity. A spokesman for the airlines said that even at the accelerated flight departure rate, it would take at least another four days to accommodate all *of the people who wanted to leave San Dominica, the Virgin Islands, Jamaica, and Haiti.*

Small curiosity. While thousands were departing from the islands, a few hundred rabid ambulance chasers arrived to witness the machete terrors.

During the first four days, more than 250 people came to San Dominica to witness the bizarre scene. Simply to be there. To watch death in action. Maybe even to get a photograph or a sound track.

CHAPTER FOURTEEN

> "I have no moral reactions anymore,"
> Damian said. "Sometimes, though, I feel a
> kind of icy, grand compassion."
>
> The Rose Diary

May 5, 1979; West Hills, San Dominica

Saturday Morning. The Fifth Day of the Season.

Peter was beginning to get his second worm's-eye view of those sneaky, dirty little wars that had come of age—or at least back into vogue—during the 1960s.

For a terrifying few minutes he had a pretty clear vision of man's inhumanity to man. Of the bizarre contrivances some men will use to gain an advantage. The horror of being alone and unknowing in the middle of terrorism and guerrilla warfare. Of being an absolute nobody in the greater scheme of things. A zero on the world's Richter scale. A gook.

A thick, dark liquid was dripping dead center on his chest. Motor oil, he realized after a few fuzzy-eyed seconds.

A train was coming!

A train was getting close to his hiding place in the West Hills' jungle. Colonel Dred's turf.

A train? Peter considered. Hiding place? He was going buggy.

He rolled over sideways and peeked through reeds of tall grass; tried to clear his sore throat of pollen and dew. Two lizards walked by at his eye level, one following the other. They seemed to be well acquainted. To be good friends, maybe lovers. . . . The two lizards stopped and played in the grass like small dinosaurs. Quite gregarious little monsters. Red bubbles throbbed under their green-and-blue chins.

Macdonald slowly rolled out, away from the BMW. He sat in the grass and picked grass and stones out of his arm and watched the sun as it peeked through trees dripping heavy moss. The sky was flaming over the leaf cover. Hot, hot, today.

Hiding out, he considered once again, trying the feeling out like a new sports coat. On the run.

After another minute massaging hopeless thoughts, Peter got up and started to make a fire. Gathered leaves and a few sticks, twigs, grass reeds, anything dry. He went over to the motorcycle and pulled out the German's dandy cross-country kit. . . . In a few minutes he'd make instant Nescafé coffee. Powdered eggs. Some kind of dried, salty beef.

Crouched over the small fire, the young man gulped down the equivalent of four eggs, the worst coffee he could imagine, mystery meat, and a chocolate bar that came all the way from West Germany *chust for such an occashun.*

While he finished the quick meal, Peter thought about Jane. He considered going into Coastown to get her. Decided against it. She was better off as far away from him as possible. Probably as far away as possible from the San Dominican police, too. For the moment Jane was fine where she was. Which was more than he could say for himself.

After he finished breakfast, he went back to the BMW's shiny black leather saddlebags. He took out a *West Point* T-shirt and unwrapped the Colt .44.

It seemed strange, unreal, as he held the old gun. He turned the chamber and saw all eight shells. He examined the gun further, remembered the army shooting ranges at West Point that were hidden in massive gray-stone buildings on a hill above the football field, Michie Stadium. He remembered a seedy shooting range inside a steaming, tin-roofed building in the Cholon section of Saigon.

Peter slowly raised the long-barreled Colt. Aimed

at a mottled banana tree leaf. Aimed at a tiny chattering yellow bird. Aimed at a small green coconut. Finally at a small black snake slithering up a gommier tree.

The tree was a good thirty-five paces away. Thirty-five yards. What pistol enthusiasts regard as trick or showboat shooting.

Looking like an old-fashioned duelist, aiming ever so carefully, Peter squeezed the trigger gently.

The distant head of the black snake exploded as if it were rotten inside. The rest of the snake dropped from the gommier like a loose vine.

In a way, the neat shot pleased and surprised him. He really hadn't expected the showpiece revolver to be so well balanced. As for the shooter—well, he knew all about the other shooter.

"Hoo boy!" Peter said out loud to the *deangerous* West Hills. "Now what, hotshot?"

CHAPTER FIFTEEN

The John Simpson Roses. Strange, blue-blood family. Damian's fourteen-year-old brother was caught cheating on a bloody exam at the Horace Mann School. Teenager swallowed half a beaker of sulfuric acid. Didn't die because the dose was so high he vomited it all up. He was crippled from his neck down, though. In an institution ever since. Damian's mother living in an institution year-round, too. Father rides round and round Manhattan and London in a big black limo provided by a multinational bank. Damian planning to kill his father in the limo one day. . . .

The Rose Diary

Mercury Landing, San Dominica

Saturday Afternoon.

The shoreline at Mercury Landing was pretty and very secluded.

Black cliffs rose high on either side of a silver of gleaming white sand. There was a glen of royal palm trees. Yellow birds. Flocks of parrots, as in an open-air pet store. A big red sun over the sea like God's angry eye.

There was a big white house over the sea, too. And on one side of the house, a dark green sedan was hidden in the shadows of casuarina trees.

There could be no doubt about one thing: San Dominica was a paradise on this earth.

Down on the beach at Mercury Landing, a man and woman were walking in the nude. Without her clothes, Carrie Rose's legs seemed a little too long, a little bowed. Her feet were slightly too large and too flat.

These were nitpicks, however, because the slender young woman was quite beautiful without clothes.

Walking beside her, Damian was almost as impressive to look at. The tall blond man wore nothing, but he had an expensive terry-cloth jumpsuit draped over one arm. He had broad shoulders and well-muscled legs. A hard, flat stomach. Pretty blond hair.

A long, sun-tanned cock hung out of the light, curly hair between Damian's legs.

"The killing should all be over now," Carrie was saying to him, with the little midwestern twang always in her voice. "It's taking too long, Damian. A week is too long."

Damian just smiled at her. He glanced out at a boat coming over a distant reef. A gray smudge on a wiggly black line. "You just want the tension you're feeling to be over," he said in a soft, detached voice. "It isn't taking too long at all. It's perfect so far. This island is as insane and paranoid as a madhouse. . . . Besides, in two days or so you get to leave. You can even start to spend all our money. Buy yourself a few cars or something, Carrie."

Carrie Rose slipped her arm around her husband's firm waist. "I want you to leave with me. I think it will be better that way. Will you do that, Damian? Leave with me?"

"If I leave"—Damian started to raise his voice—"then Campbell and Harold Hill will come looking for us. Sooner or later they'll find us. Suddenly a big black car will arrive at our villa somewhere or other. Their short-haired killers will come down on us like little Nazis. Kill us. Become heroes. Write books and make movies like *The French Connection*.

"Look at how it's growing." Damian suddenly changed moods, smiled unexpectedly. "Irreverent little beast. *Big* beast."

As he was talking, his penis had extended itself straight out and to the left. Blood had gone to its tip—which was just touching Carrie's bare leg.

She pushed it away. "If I have to tell you everything explicitly, I'm frightened this time. You're playing too many games this time. I don't want us to end like this. . . . You mentioned little Nazis before. Well, we're going to be searched for like Nazis."

Damian threw up his arms like a Frenchman. "Let them search. Let them search. They looked for Eichmann for twenty years. They're stupid, Carrie. Remember that. They are all stupid, bumbling idiots."

Carrie just bowed her head. She let her long hair swing from side to side, brushing over her breasts.

For the next few minutes they walked along the lip of the cove in silence.

"If I were to lie down in the water there?" She finally spoke. . . .

The two beautiful people walked to where the white sand was slicked-over wet. Damian put down the expensive terry-cloth suit, and Carrie lay on it. Damian kneeled over her—began to lower himself slowly. For a fleeting moment his clear blue eyes seemed almost gentle to her.

"So tell me, Carrie," he said, "how was your handsome stockbroker?"

Saturday Evening.

The main coup de theatre was staged that night, Saturday, May 5.

At eleven o'clock automobile headlights appeared at Mercury Landing's high, silver-painted front gates. Emerging from the shadowy gates, the Cuban waved the first car on.

Standing at the other end of the driveway, Damian Rose could hear gravel being crushed under heavy automobile tires.

One hour late, but they were coming, anyway.

The tall blond man checked a Smith & Wesson revolver under his suit jacket. A small snub-nosed .38. A very appropriate weapon for the evening's performance, Rose thought. . . . Tonight he was going to play Hammett for the locals.

As he continued to watch down the hill, a second and third set of headlights turned onto the pitch-black driveway. One pair of lights was outrageously cross-eyed. It exposed tall Bermuda grass on one side of the car, palm trees and purplish sky on the other.

The three cars completely disappeared for a moment. They passed behind bay trees and bushes called fire-of-the-forest, where six local gunmen had been told to wait. Just wait.

Then bright headlights sprayed all over the vined walls and windows of the whitewashed main house. The cars began to park in a glen of casuarinas in front of the villa.

Ready or not, Damian thought to himself, this is it. Curtain time.

He rehearsed all his lines one final time before he had to go on.

Out on a large flagstone terrace at the rear of the villa, Kingfish Toone could be heard speaking pidgin English with a French-Congolese accent.

"We are prepare to offer you cash only," the broad-shouldered mercenary explained to the four guerrilla leaders who had just arrived. "One hundred twenty-five thousand. You could buy whatever you like with the money. Guns. Whatever you like. That is my final offer, Colonel."

Dassie "Monkey" Dred let his pretty chocolate face fall between his long legs. His long cornbraids fell. He began to laugh in a loud, crude voice.

Then he started making bird noises out on the terrace.

"Ayeee! S'mady take dis monkey-mahn away fram me," Dred said to no one in particular. "Dis Africahn smell lak hairdresser fram Americah."

Kingfish Toone smiled along with Dred's men. The African had met and dealt with this type of madman before.

Across the terrace, the Cuban sat on a small wicker rocking chair, saying nothing at all.

"That smell is something called soap. You've never smelled soap before, have you?"

A tall white man spoke from the doorway leading back into the house. His blond hair was all wet, slicked back close to the scalp, like something out of *Esquire* or *Gentlemen's Quarterly*. He was wearing an expensively tailored cream gabardine suit. Appropriate accoutrements, perfectly matched. An inlaid ivory watch. An ivory ring. A black Gucci belt and Gucci loafers.

Damian Rose ran his hand back over his wet hair once again. Then he crossed the patio to the young, bearded revolutionary. As he walked, his jacket swung open, revealing a fancy belt holster and the Smith & Wesson.

"Colonel Dred." Damian smiled like a Clint Eastwood character. "Your work is admired far off this island. In Europe, I'm talking about. In black America."

The guerrilla soldier's face softened for a split second that wasn't lost on Rose. Then Dred dismissed the compliment with a wave of his hand. He spit on the terrace.

"Yo' very well-train ape"—he indicated Kingfish Toone sitting across the terrace—"has offered me—what is it?—cash. . . . I don't need dat. I have all kind cash from ganja sellin'."

Rose's soft blue eyes never left the much darker eyes of the San Dominican. "First of all, my 'well-trained ape' could rip off your coconuts in about five seconds' time, Colonel. Secondly, whatever your problem is, we can find a solution."

"He wants the guns used in this raid." The Cuban spoke in Spanish from his seat across the terrace. "He has trouble buying guns."

"For obvious reasons." Damian turned back to Dred. "I don't want to arm you that well, Colonel. . . . You may have the guns, however. We'll give you two hundred fifty M-16's. Plus handguns."

"Fifty t'ousan' rounds of ammunition. At least fifty machine guns," Dred shouted. His three officers smiled and clapped their hands like Barnum and Bailey chimps.

The lips of the tall blond man parted in a slight smile. He slid his hands back over the wet hair again. He took out a pack of English cigarettes.

"I can't give you the machine guns," Damian said flatly.

Suddenly Monkey Dred was on his feet, shouting at the top of his lungs. His cornbraids shook like a hundred dancing black snakes. A U.S. Army ammunition belt around his waist jounced and jangled.

"Forty machine guns, den! Deliver at least one day before dat *massacree.*"

Damian Rose picked up a camphor candle from a patio table. He lit his cigarette with it. The word *massacree* rolled over his tongue. *Massacree.*

"One fifty-millimeter machine gun. For you!" Rose let the cigarette dangle. "But the other guns to be distributed *right now.* Plus a bonus of twenty-five thousand rounds of ammunition. . . . If I could offer you more, I would. It's not my money, Colonel. . . . Our friends in Cuba know what you need, and what you don't."

A loud laugh came up from somewhere deep in the black man's chest. "All right, den!" he shouted.

Damian Rose smiled. Friends in Cuba indeed . . . he'd won. Massacree!

He heaved the red jar and camphor candle far down the hillside toward the Caribbean. The lamp hit a distant, invisible rock. It broke with the pop of a light bulb.

Just after it hit, lights flashed on and off down on the water. A small motor boat started to come in toward shore.

Carrie.

"Your guns, Colonel," Damian Rose announced. "Enough guns and ammunition to take over the entire island . . . if you'll listen to just a bit of advice."

* * *

As early as 6:00 A.M. on the sixth day, there were bold, unnerving machete murders in the two most expensive hotels in San Dominica's two principal cities.

In Coastown, a young fashion photographer from Greenwich, Connecticut, was found floating face-down in a pretty courtyard swimming pool in the Princess Hotel. A black-handled sugar-cane machete was sticking out of the man's back like an exclamation point to the crime.

In Port Gerry, an English barrister's wife was hacked to pieces while she was gathering hibiscus in the garden of the exclusive Spice Point Inn. The woman was then bundled up in Spice Point towels and thrown onto the inn's dining veranda by fleeing, half-naked black men.

Also very early in the morning, both the Gleaner and the Evening Star received Dead Letters. In these new communications, Colonel Dred claimed responsibility for the morning's hotel murders.

Dred also warned that the rate of race killings on San Dominica would escalate by 1,000 percent daily until an interest in all hotels, restaurants, and other major businesses was turned over to the people.

Someone at the Gleaner calculated that since four people had died so far on the fifth, a minimum of forty people had to die on May 6.

Then four hundred . . . then four thousand . . .

May 6, 1979, Sunday
Princess,
Spice Point,
Hit

CHAPTER SIXTEEN

> We're conditioned to expect things to
> happen at a certain rate. To have a certain
> rhythm. What we did on San Dominica
> was to take all of the prevailing rhythms
> away.
>
> The Rose Diary

May 6, 1979, Coastown, San Dominica

Sunday Morning. The Sixth Day of the Season.

At 7:15 the morning of the sixth day, Peter Macdonald stepped through the kitchen door of Brooks Campbell's expensive villa in Coastown, shouted, "Scrambled eggs!" and knocked the handsome CIA man down with a hard, right-handed punch to his Greco-Roman nose.

"You better stay right down there," Peter yelled

as Campbell tried to push himself to his feet. He took out the Colt .44 and pointed the barrel at an imaginary target, one-half inch in circumference, centered between Campbell's hazel-brown eyes.

"What the hell do you want?"

"Just the truth," Peter said quietly. "I'm not going to go into what's happened to me since the last time you fucked me over—how I came to sleep in your garage last night—but I want to know everything you know about the machete murders. I want to know all your so-called state secrets."

Very slowly, cautiously, Campbell got to his feet. "There's only one problem with what you're saying," he said to Peter. "I just don't believe you'd shoot me. I know you wouldn't."

The next thing Brooks Campbell saw was the big steel handle of the Colt .44. It struck him sideways across the cheekbone, and he crashed down on the yellow tile floor again.

"You *will* believe I'll shoot you in a minute," he heard dimly. A brown workboot stamped down hard on his chest, then he was pulled up roughly by his hair. Suddenly he felt a hot streak go down the right side of his face.

"Now, dammit, you better talk to me, mister. I know how to do shit like this. Torturing men. Believe me I do."

Campbell was beginning to focus in on the heat burner of his own kitchen stove. The coil was red hot—a glowing orange—and his hair was starting to smoke. Bacon cooking on another burner was spitting all over the other side of his face.

"I swear to God I'll fry your goddamn ear!" Macdonald yelled at him, army drill instructor style.

"We know the Mafia is involved somehow!" Campbell finally screamed out. "Let me up. I'm burning, Macdonald!"

Peter loosened his stranglehold, but not so much that Campbell could get up. "I don't know what that's supposed to mean. The Mafia . . . the Mafia what?"

"They've been trying to get the assembly here to legalize casino gambling for years. . . . Now they're going to get what they want—or they say they'll destroy this place. Blow up San Dominica and write it off as a tax loss. . . . That's all we know. I swear it. Macdonald, I'm on fire!"

Peter finally let go of Campbell. What he'd heard started to make a little sense. It explained some of the things that had happened.

"What does Colonel Dred have to do with that? With the Mafia? Casino gambling?"

The CIA man was holding his ear as if it had been bitten into. He was wearing a gold-and-red dragon kimono, and for once in his life Brooks Campbell looked ridiculous.

"We don't know how or even *if* they got to Dred." He continued to tell half-truths with some conviction. "Apparently, something big is coming up soon. Those letters in the newspapers are actually warnings to the assembly. Some big horror show is coming. What you don't understand is that we're all going wild trying to stop it from happening."

"I'm getting a feeling that you're lying again," Peter said. He opened the refrigerator and looked inside. He threw Campbell some ice for the bruise on his face. Then he took a long, sloppy swig of orange juice from an open jug.

"All right." He waved the cowboy pistol at Campbell. "This has been a little better than our first talk, I guess. I'll be back if I need to know anything else from you. Just don't ever make the mistake of thinking that I wouldn't shoot you. I'd shoot you. I don't even like you."

Peter backed out the kitchen door, then ran to the BMW.

Now what kind of horror show could be coming up? he wondered as he eased the motorcycle down palm-lined lanes and backed out toward the rain forest. Would the Mafia get mixed up in something like this? And how does the blond man fit in? A mercenary? To do what?

But, Christ, this was a hell of a lot better than being a bartender for a nutty German storm trooper. . . . Maybe he should become a cop, or a Philip Marlowe–type detective or something. Someday soon. . . .

After his success with Campbell, Peter was at least feeling alive again. That was a start.

Coastown, San Dominica

A seagull flapped up Parmenter Street. Dipped to scrutinize natives setting up a brightly colored fruit mart. Angled right shoulder, wing first, and glided like a clever wooden airplane over the exclusive crimson-roofed Coastown Princess Hotel.

Sitting pretty with a big supply of steaming coffee, kipper and eggs, fresh rolls and sweet butter, Carrie Rose was out on her loggia at the Princess.

She was just beginning to compose a long, personal entry in the million-dollar diary. When she wrote, she told about a particular late summer afternoon in Paris. An afternoon that had provided a key to the whole thing.

August 10, 1978; Paris

The place was called Atlantic City, and it was a trendy little bistro recently sprung up as a haven for Americans on the avenue Marceau.

The cafe was already famous for its twelve varieties of *le hamburger*. And, to a lesser extent, for its big wooden posters illustrating different trivial points about a seedy boardwalk resort in southeastern New Jersey.

DID YOU KNOW THAT?
THE FIRST EASTER PARADE IN AMERICA
WAS HELD IN ATLANTIC CITY . . .
THE FIRST FERRIS WHEEL WAS OPERATED IN ATLANTIC CITY. . . .
THE FIRST MOTION PICTURE WAS MADE
IN ATLANTIC CITY. . . .
THE FIRST PICTURE POSTCARDS WERE
FROM ATLANTIC CITY. . . .

Floppy white hat covering half of her face, Carrie Rose walked back slowly into the dark bar. She heard "Lady Marmalade" playing on the jukebox. *"Voulez-vous coucher avec moi? . . ."*

White butterfly stockings swished softly as she continued until she saw the wheelchair. Then Carrie realized that, for the first time in a long time, she was frightened.

"The incomparable, infamous Mrs. Rose." Nickie Handy spoke to her from the corner of a candlelit booth. "Now what could your pleasure be this lovely, shitty afternoon?"

As Carrie slid into the oaken booth, she kissed the top of Nickie's head. Her ex-partner. Then, as she settled in across from her old friend, she couldn't help staring at the crippled man's face.

Nickie Handy, still not thirty years old, had no left cheek now. No left side to his face. Just sagging flesh hanging off a cheekbone.

"I should come see you more than this," she said softly. "Both Damian and I are rats, Nickie. We really are bad."

A waitress came and Carrie ordered a bottle of pouilly-fuissé. Nickie made a remark about the French girl's breasts. "Sow's teats," he said with a crooked little smile.

"Let's have it. Let's have it." He turned back to Carrie. "Don't hand me this visiting-the-local-VFW crap. Buying your hot-shit wines and all that. . . ."

"All right. I came to talk to you about the shooting. Saigon."

A surprised look dropped over Nickie Handy's sad, Quasimodo face. "Let's not," he said. Then suddenly his face twisted up like a pretzel and he raised his voice.

"You're looking at me like a fucking cat, Carrie. That disdainful look Siamese cats get. Bee-utiful! I love it, you cunt."

"You're paranoid." Carrie continued to speak softly, almost lovingly. "Damian and I are doing a job with Harold Hill. Harry the Hack and your *very good friend* Brooks Campbell. Who would you suggest we go talk to?"

The cripple took his mug of beer and slowly

spilled it out onto the pine-and-sawdust floor. "Bee-utiful!"

"Hey! Hey! Hey!" a dark-bearded French bartender called back. "Behave yourself, Nickee!"

Handy screwed up his face again. Some kind of awful tic, apparently.

"Brooks Campbell was supposed to be paying me in that alley in Saigon. Blew my head off instead. Hello, Nick. *Blam! Blam! Blam!* . . . Left me for a fucking cold stiff in the sewer, Carrie.

"Dead chink mouse floated past my nose. I thought I was in hell already. Crippled in the sewer. Face messed up like it is. *Your new partners, you say?*"

"There was no provocation for what they did, Nickie? Privateering? . . . It was just a double cross?"

"Straight double cross! Me and a poor gook bastard. I think he even kept my money for himself. Brooks Campbell. Fucking movie-star face."

"Those awful bastards, Nickie."

"Your partners," Nickie said again. "I love it! I love it!"

Carrie and the crippled man sat drinking in the Americanized bar until after five o'clock. At that point American business types began to crowd inside. Tourists and backpacking hippies from the nearby L'Etoile. By 5:30 it was impossible to hear a normal conversation inside the tacky bistro.

Saying something about cigarettes, Carrie reached inside her shoulder bag. Then she leaned over deep into the dark booth and shot Nickie Handy dead. Two soft little *pfftts* that were never heard over the din. Heart shots. Quicklike, because she didn't want him to hurt.

Nickie lay down on the scarred wooden table like a good little drunk.

Carrie's mind was racing as she elbowed her way out and onto the avenue. Two very good reasons for the murder.

First of all, poor Nickie was one of the few people left who could still identify her and Damian. Second, she'd liked Nickie too much to let him live like that. To let him go where he was obviously going.

Slightly dizzy from the bar scene, she crossed the avenue Marceau in a sea of Renaults, Simcas, wolf whistles. Up some side street. Stacked heels clicking, white butterfly stockings singing silk.

She took off the floppy white Easter bonnet. Tossed it over a slat fence into somebody's yard. She took off the uncomfortable high-heeled pumps and got into the black flats that were in her shoulder bag.

At avenue Montaigne, she met Damian. The two of them embraced for a long moment. Then the pretty young couple walked arm in arm across the murky, slow-moving Seine.

Almost at once, they began to prepare to be double-crossed.

CHAPTER SEVENTEEN

> The effect that we wanted most on San
> Dominica was helpless confusion. A
> feeling like darkness and light being
> turned on and off at our will. Things
> suddenly being dangerous that weren't
> supposed to be dangerous. . . . More
> important, there had to be no way to chart
> any of it. No known patterns.
>
> The Rose Diary

Wylde's Fall, San Dominica

Between seven Sunday morning and the late afternoon, nothing happened on San Dominica that
hadn't been happening for the previous thousand
years or so. The more than 150 beaches were pearly
white, striking, and perfect; the royal blue skies
were clear and pure—a 1,000 percent improvement

on any metropolitan sky; the sunshine was uninterrupted.

And while nothing terrifying was happening, the Americans and Europeans still on the island had time to sit back and think about what had happened. Not least of all, the sixty-one members of the government assembly had time to consider their unlucky alternatives for the future.

At four in the afternoon, Colonel Dassie Dred stood on the verge of worldwide fame.

Looking down from the second highest and most beautiful waterfall in the Caribbean—Wylde's Falls—he could see a barefoot black boy and a white couple making the popular walking tour up the many-tiered water shoots.

The three people sloshed through the most beautiful, black, freshwater pools. They splashed together in cascading ten- and twenty-foot-high falls; occasionally shouted to one another over the crashing roar of the blue water; stopped once for a misty camera shot.

When the young guide finally turned the rocky corner beneath his hiding place, Dred extended his hand through a clump of bushes. The small boy allowed himself to be pulled up, leaving the white couple looking up at the leering face of the revolutionary. "Yo' go home now," Dred said to the boy. "Nemmine be lookin' back."

As he spoke, two of his men jumped through

banana leaves into the bubbly pool below. One man came swinging a cane machete sideways like a baseball bat.

The long knife caught a screaming, thirtyish-looking woman across the front of her *Town & Country* summer blouse. The hard blow upended her in a clumsy three-point fall.

The second, stronger soldier brought his knife straight down. The woman's blond, bankerish-looking husband stood still for a moment, then he split from the shoulders down and toppled over Wylde's Falls.

Meanwhile, down at the park's entry gates, a handful of tourists and lounging guides were watching the day's final climbers make their way down the tricky falls. As they watched two couples and their guides climb down slowly, a body—a swimming woman, it looked like—shot headfirst around a high curve in the swift water. The swimming woman disappeared again; then toppled over a smooth lip of the black rock; then caught sideways up against a jutting boulder shooting bubbly white water high in the air.

A man split like broken scissors came down next. The body made it around the jutting rock, bounced down several small falls, skimmed past the terror-stricken crowd at the gates, then disappeared without a sound into the sea.

Colonel Dred had conducted his first official machete raid, and as it had been skillfully designed to be, it was the very best one so far.

Dred was ready.

Trelawney, San Dominica

Sunday Evening.

A greasy dish of sticky brown rice sat in front of him. Gray shredded goat. Some shellfish that wasn't lobster, wasn't crab or shrimp, wasn't really edible.

Peter Macdonald thought he saw a small black claw rise up and swim in the stew. He gobbled it up. It was sixty cents for the meal and green tea—a bargain.

After his Sunday dinner, Macdonald sat in a dark rear corner of the native restaurant. He slowly smoked two cigarettes. He nervously pushed his hand back through his hair twenty or thirty times within five minutes or less.

Sitting there all alone, Peter remembered a dumb movie he'd seen once. Some handsome blond actor had played a man who'd simply gone to *The New York Times* to get out of a pack of trouble. Gone to the *Times* the way people used to go to the police—and the next thing you knew, everything was copacetic. The man in the movie was safe and sound.

The screen credits rolled up over the man's frozen, smiling face. "America the Beautiful" played. Everybody in the theater went home as happy as clams.

Idle speculations of a drowning man.

Because what exactly could *he* tell *The New York Times*? Peter had begun to speculate. What could he tell anybody, really? That he'd seen this tall blond Englishman—maybe an Englishman—in the vicinity of *one* of the San Dominica machete murders? That he'd held a State Department man's face to the burner of an electric stove, and the man had begun to scream about the Mafia?

Suddenly the restaurant's waitress and cook were standing over him. A small, moon-faced black girl, she'd been flitting all night around the main room like a trapped moth. Table . . . table . . . window . . . stove . . . table . . . window.

Nobody would let the moth-girl out, though . . . table.

"Yo' lak yo' lobster, yes, mahn?" Loose translation: You're crazy to eat in here. Let me outside, please. I'm a moth.

Peter smiled at the moth thought; at something in the young girl's eyes. "Good food," he said softly. "Better than at the big hotels."

The waitress remembered the words later for the San Dominica police. She said that the young American left the restaurant around nine. That he'd gotten on a motorcycle outside.

The police told her that the American man had gone a little crazy on account of all the murders. They said they wanted him for questioning. Nothing serious.

Coastown, San Dominica

Almost simultaneously with the police interview in the Trelawney restaurant, four men in expensive raw-silk suits—Park Avenue bankers, from the look of them—sat down to dinner on a handsome screened-in porch on the big estate in Coastown proper.

The four were San Dominica's prime minister, Joe Walthey; Great Western Air Transport's Brooks Campbell; the Forlenza Family's Isadore Goldman; and Goldman's man on San Dominica, a beachboy type by the name of Duane Nicholson.

The meal that the four men were served began with Chincoteagues; then a Montrachet; stuffed lamb *en ballon*; buttered celery; corn. In the wings was a grand floating island.

All in all, a most delicious, civilized feast.

On and off, the men watched the leggy mistress of Prime Minister Walthey swimming laps in the blue-bottomed pool that stretched out directly in front of the porch.

On and off, Izzie Goldman tried to explain the facts of life and death to the other three. A thin, liver-spotted hand floated out in front of the gangster as he spoke.

"I'm seventy-four years old," he said quietly, so that they all had to concentrate on his words. "I don't understand why you ask me all these schoolboy questions about the Roses." Goldman sighed. "Why can't you let them do their work? Pay the money and forget about it."

"Because they're a liability," Brooks Campbell said to him. "Because I have my orders from way, way up the ladder."

The old man took a bird bite of his lamb. "They're too smart to carry tales." He talked and chewed. "I don't understand why everybody is trying so hard to make another Bay of Pigs catastrophe here."

"This is hardly the liberation of Cuba." Campbell pointed a finger at the old man. "And besides, I think Rose has gone crazy. We never saw any plans like this. A few murders, yes. Massacres, no."

The prime minister of San Dominica brushed a fly away from his wine.

Joseph Walthey, "Jose," was a short, stocky

black. Forty-one years old. A demagogue and potentially a dictator. The black man had a neat pencil mustache, a big thumb of a nose, a very bumpy, pocked complexion.

"Just for the sake of . . . dinner talk"—he spoke with a soft, diplomatic lilt—"why won't you answer a few of our questions, Mr. Goldman? What possible harm could come from ridding the world of these two murderers, for example?"

The old man sank even farther into his big rattan chair. His gray suit coat bunched terribly around a pink-and-brown silk tie. Pink flamingos were crushed all over the tie.

The prime minister's girlfriend dived into the pool again, and Izzie Goldman heard an insane old song start up in his mind.

Hubba hubba, ding ding
Baby, you got everything
What a face, what a figger!
What a shame that you're a
nigger!

Vaude-ville—bring it back! Please! Quick!

"Above and beyond everything else that was wrong here"—he glanced across the table at Brooks Campbell—"I don't think you'll catch them. Let them go back to France, Mr. Campbell. Prime Minister. Let it end after tomorrow. Trust me on this."

To his immediate left, Duane Nicholson sat flicking ashes from his cigarette into his empty dinner plate.

"No. We want the Roses dead," Brooks Campbell repeated. "That's our position."

Isadore Goldman stared at the beachboy Nicholson before making his next statement on the matter. "The people who put their cigarettes in their plates," the old man finally said, "should have to eat out of their ashtrays."

And those were absolutely Isadore Goldman's last words on the fiasco.

Trelawney, San Dominica

A little after nine, Peter Macdonald hid the BMW motorcycle in thick brush, then walked inside the Trelawney bus station.

The station was one small, dim room that smelled as if an army had stopped to urinate and delouse there.

Peter examined a schedule for buses going across the island to Port Gerry. At Port Gerry, he thought he had a way to get off San Dominica safely. A way to get some help. Maybe. The question was whether to travel anonymously by bus or quickly by bike.

None of the hang-arounds inside the station

seemed to be noticing him, he believed. That was good, at least.

He sat down on one of the long gray benches. Saw a newspaper headline crumpled up under another seat. DOUBLE MURDERS! DRED ON THE MOVE.

Almost 9:15 now . . . starting to miss Jane like hell. Remembering what it was like to be lonely.

He began to read a six-foot-high-by-ten-foot-wide community blackboard. A child's handwriting, it looked like.

NOW THAT ELECTION RESULTS ALL OVER THE CARIBBEAN HAVE TURNED OUT VICTORIOUS FOR SOCIALISTS, AND JOE IS SERIOUSLY ILL, I THINK WE SHOULD TAKE A LONG LOOK AT COMING ELECTIONS.

JOE'S PLAYBOY ATTITUDE IS UNBECOMING AN EXECUTIVE TO OFFICE. PROFESSOR SAM HAS ONLY FOUR YEARS OF SCHOOLING (CHECK RECORDS OF THE BAINTY SCHOOL IN COASTOWN), WHILE I AM, AS YOU KNOW, GRADUATE OF THE UNIVERSITY OF THE WEST INDIES.

THOSE OF YOU WHO VOTE FOR "JOE" ARE VOTING FOR THE FOL-

LOWING: MORE CONTROL BY FOR-
EIGNERS, CIA, HIGH PRICES, LOW
WAGES, MORE CONTROL BY FOR-
EIGNERS, WILDNESS IN STREET BY
COLONEL DRED, NO PRICE CON-
TROLS, UNSANITARY—WITH FOOD
SPREAD ON THE GROUND WHERE
WE WALK, SPIT, ETC., TO BE SOLD
TO CONSUMERS. MORE CONTROL
BY FOREIGNERS. EVEN DRED HIM-
SELF WOULD BE PREFERRED BET-
TER THAN OLD BLACK "JOE."

TOMMY (THOMAS WYASS)

Macdonald the sign reader. Looking for direction? Clues? More control by foreigners. Prime
Minister Joe Walthey. Dred on move.

Peter read: FORBIDDEN IN THIS TERMINAL:
SMOKING, SCREAMING, OBSCENE LAN-
GUAGE, SHELLING OF PEANUTS, EATING
OF CHEWING GUM. THANK YOU. TOMMY.

Peter was chewing gum, smoking, screaming obscene language inside his brain. He went into a dark
wooden phone booth, where he could chew and
smoke his brains out in peace.

He thought about where he ought to spend the
night. Port Gerry? The woods again? . . . No one
ever teaches you how to survive in America. Not

even the army, really. They just teach the army how to survive.

Finally, against all his previous resolves, against his whole idea of trying to keep her out of this, Peter decided that he had to call Jane.

First he called her friends in Coastown. She left, they told him. Jane had gone back to the inn. Shit. Shit. Shit. Shit.

Peter made the call to Turtle Bay. Number ninety. The Plantation Inn. Switchboard operator. "Cottage number fourteen, please. . . . Jane, it's me. Peter. I've been trying to call you all day in Coastown."

"Oh, Peter! Where are you?"

There was a short pause at his end of the line.

"I want you to go back to the States," Peter finally said. "See what Westerhuis can do to get you on a flight out of here. . . . Janie?"

"Dammit all to hell, Macdonald! Tell me where you are. Cool it, Peter."

Peter smiled for a second. That was Jane. He stopped the melodramatics and told her where he'd been for the past day. Then he told her what he thought they ought to do now. What they shouldn't do. Only after he'd gone through it all—the talk about himself—did Jane mention the blond Englishman.

"He was here, Peter."

Small, shocking statement. *He was here.*

"I saw him this afternoon. I think . . . it had to be him. He was blond, maybe six feet two . . ."

Peter stopped her. Suddenly it was as if he were a combat officer again, giving orders that must be followed. "I want you to lock and latch all the doors and windows right now, Jane."

"*Everything is locked.* Just come and get me."

He tried to visualize the room. The cottage itself. Fool's Hot Toast. He tried to imagine how he would go about attacking it. Defending it.

"All right, that's good. Will you turn off all the lights in there? Do it right now, okay?"

"Okay! Okay!"

He heard the sound of the phone being set down.

He'd been right there. Peter considered again. Came down into the inn as if he had some kind of diplomatic immunity. Brass balls, at least.

Suddenly he had a quick flash of the tall blond figure standing over Turtle Bay four days earlier. Looking as if he owned the place. Looking as if he owned the goddamn world.

Then Jane was back on the phone. Whispering, all of a sudden.

"It's pitch black in here," she told him. "I can see a couple walking out on the beach. Oh, Peter, this is so creepy I don't believe it's happening."

"For what it's worth," Peter said, "I'm on my way."

Turtle Bay, San Dominica

The sound outside cottage number fourteen was something like *bomp*.

Bomp, *bomp* . . . *bomp*, *bomp*, *bomp*.

The noise stopped suddenly, and Jane Cooke stood perfectly still, quiet and afraid, inside the dark bedroom. First she caught her breath, then she tried to figure out the sound.

Rose apples—she finally solved the small mystery. The noise was rose apples dropping onto the bungalow roof.

Jane realized that she was letting herself get a little confused now. Stop it. Grab control.

One of her hands slid along the cool limestone wall. Her cheek pressed lightly against the wall. Long blond hair brushed against it. Her fingers groped along the sloppily laid wallpaper. Ruffles. Air pockets. Then an end to the wall altogether . . . doorjamb . . . gritty bathroom tile.

She put her face under the faucet. Soaked herself. Drank some rusty-tasting water. Then she put down the toilet seat cover and sat. Took cigarettes out of her T-shirt pocket. Looked down and saw the dark outline of a book on the floor. *All the President's Men*. Their bathroom book.

She smoked three cigarettes while thinking about her and Peter's situation. She heard another small noise . . . beetles flying against the window. *Woof!*

Like getting punched in the stomach. She decided she ought to be out where she could at least watch the front window.

The big window at the front of the bungalow was showing a crystal-clear black-and-white movie.

No more couple walking on the beach . . . thin, smoky, purplish clouds drifted past a full moon. Old, shriveled night clouds. A low line of frothy white surf running around the cove, outlining it like whipped cream.

She'd been all right until Peter called, Jane started to think. . . .

A lot of men had ogled her around the inn. Even tall blond ones. Even tall blond ones who *might* look a little English. . . .

Nice girl from the capital of South Dakota, she thought. . . . Boyfriend accidentally witnessed a murder. Just a glance. No more than ten seconds! Must be an Alfred Hitchcock film . . . macabre throughout, ghoulish like *Frenzy*, but a happy ending. Ingrid Bergman and Cary Grant clink champagne glasses, then kiss.

Thinking about the tall blond Englishman again. *The Tall Blond Englishman*. Couldn't keep her hands from shaking now. Funny—*odd*, that is. He'd been drinking by himself on the Pineapple Terrace. A very good-looking, serious man. Nice tan. Black wraparound glasses that made her think of the Mediterranean. She thought he'd been watching her while she taught a little girl how to get water out of her ear. "First, hop on the foot opposite the clogged-up ear. Here—like this, silly-face. Now. Bang the side of your head. Bang it good. . . ."

After that, she was *sure* the blond man was following her. Keeping her in sight, anyway. Well, he *seemed* to be. . . .

Jane looked down at her watch. Glowing red numbers in the dark bedroom: 10:43. An hour and ten minutes had passed since Peter had called. Usually the ride from Coastown took just over an hour. Add five minutes more from Trelawney.

Standing there beside the dark front window, she heard another onslaught of apples on the roof. More blasted rose apples.

Then footsteps.

Then a young woman was outside, calling her name at the front door. . . .

And then one of the shuttered windows was being broken down with something sharp and powerful like an ax.

May 7, 1979, Monday
Massacre
at
Elizabeth's
Fancy

CHAPTER EIGHTEEN

> The planning is usually interesting. Getting
> close to the final time is interesting. But
> the climax, the big kill, was usually
> something of an <u>anti</u>climax . . . not to the
> victims, of course.
>
> The Rose Diary

May 7, 1979; Mandeville, San Dominica

Monday Morning. The Seventh Day of the Season.

At 4:00 A.M. on the seventh day, Jane's eyes popped open wide.

She saw nothing at first. Then the long shadow of a man sitting by her bed. Then bright afterimages of running men and machetes. And a tall woman who spoke very sweetly, as if she were Jane's best friend.

As she began to scream, a night lamp clicked on. A shiny aluminum lamp nailed to the wall. The man sitting underneath the light was the chief of police. He had a small black pipe stuck in his mouth. A holster and gun were slung over his short-sleeved white shirt.

"*Shhhhhh* . . . you're in the Mandeville Hospital," he whispered to the blond girl. "You're all right. Everything is all right now."

The black man smiled and winked at her, then he clicked the light off.

Jane lay in the dark, shivering badly. Her teeth began chattering, and she started to cry. Thought about Peter. Just wanted to hold tight. Hold tight.

"*What is happening?*"

She wasn't sure whether she'd *said* the words out loud or just *thought* them loud. She started to shiver; then to cry; then to hug herself because it was so damn awful.

Then she was asleep again.

In her dreams they came to the hospital for her. They came somewhere for her. The two black men. The tall blond man with the wraparound sunglasses. The young woman. . . . They kept screaming at her to tell them where Peter was. . . . "*I don't know! I don't know! Please don't hurt me.*"

The heavyset black police chief smiled at her. He put his forefinger to his lips. Made a little fire in the bowl of his black pipe.

"*Shhhh. Shhhh*. No one can hurt you now," Dr. Johnson said.

Even though the worst day of the season of the machete had begun.

Cape John, San Dominica

Monday Afternoon.

Like a white kite in the wind, a seagull swung back and forth high over his head.

Aaaaa! Aaaaa! Aaaaa!

Lying in a buttery midday sun, Damian felt a wonderful calm begin to drift over him. He and Carrie were approaching a definite benchmark now. The last of the island's terrors.

Ah—there was nothing like being in the sun for reviving one's prospects.

He could feel the salt water drying on his face and legs. The hot sun broiled him in a way that made it seem rather fun.

For perhaps the five hundredth time, Damian reviewed the final details in his mind.

The *massacree*.

Carrie's, then his own, escape.

There would be no Nickie Handy–style double crosses this time out. No meeting up with Brooks Campbell or Harold Hill in dark, deserted alleyways. All that was left for him now was to set out a last tasty morsel of bait for Great Western Air Transport. Something for King Rat Brooks Campbell to nibble on.

Then a check on the plot's final playing piece—a tricky strong-arm killer named Clive Lawson.

Then it was home again, home again, jiggity jog.

Mandeville, San Dominica

At 1:00 P.M. a man in a summer sports coat and white hat took a deep breath, then approached an old woman wearing a Red Cross hat who sat at the first-floor reception desk inside the Mandeville Hospital.

"My name is Max Westerhuis," the man announced in an impatient, self-important tone. "I'm told I have to come to this desk to get a pass to see Miss Cooke."

The elderly nurse reached into her desk drawer. She took out a plain brown clipboard. She checked a list of visitors cleared to see hospital patients that was written on sheets of paper attached to the board. There was only one visitor cleared for Miss J. Cooke in room 206.

The nurse wrote out a slip for Maximilian Westerhuis, manager of the Plantation Inn.

As the policeman posted at room 206 opened the

door for him, the man in the white hat put a finger to his lips. "Miss Cooke," he said in the same official tone he'd used at the front desk.

"Peter," Jane whispered as soon as he'd closed the door behind him.

She looked very pale and shaken to him. Large gauze bandages were wrapped around her neck and both arms; an intravenous bottle hung over the bed.

Peter went to her and they held each other tightly, saying things that should have been said long before then, expressing feelings they'd both been afraid of.

As they finally pulled apart, Jane began to tell him about the three people who'd come to their cottage at the Plantation Inn. How they'd wanted to know where he was hiding. All the things they'd done to try to make her talk. . . . For his part, Peter told Jane about his surprise visit at Brooks Campbell's; the Mafia connection; the big blowup that was apparently coming soon.

"Well, what do we do now?"

"The first thing—I want to get you out of this hospital. We must be dealing with a black version of the Keystone Kops here. Look at how easily I got in."

"Peter, if they'd been after me—*they had me* last night. All they wanted to know was where *you* were."

"That doesn't make complete sense. If you did

see him yesterday, they'd want you, too. Wouldn't they? Oh, hell, I don't know what's going on around here.''

The young man sat down on the hospital bed. His shoulders began to sag. His neck muscles felt unbelievably tense and twisted.

''Peter, did you see anything that day *besides* the blond man?''

''I don't know. I don't think I did. . . . The best solution I can come up with,'' Peter finally said, ''is that we both have to get off San Dominica. I want to try Washington.'' He looked at Jane. ''Will you meet me there? In a day—a few days. There's a hotel in Washington called the Hay-Adams. It's right across from the White House.''

For the first time that afternoon, Jane smiled. ''Good. Then we can take this thing right to the top. We can't do any worse than at the U.S. embassy, right?'' She kissed him hard, then rested her head on his shoulder. ''Darling Max.''

''Somebody's going to listen to us. It can't be this unbelievably fucked-up everywhere.''

Jane smiled again. ''Maximilian Westerhuis! God, Peter.''

They both started to laugh, hushing each other so the guard wouldn't come in. Then they hugged again, secured their pact to meet in Washington by

Wednesday. Peter left the hospital the very same way he'd originally come in.

Much, much too easily.

Coastown, San Dominica

Inside the Princess Hotel, meanwhile, Carrie sat with the gleaming white doors to her loggia flung open wide. Bright sunshine and a sympathetic breeze drifted in. Smells of fresh flowers came up from a pretty glen two stories below.

Carrie stared hard at the garish face looking back at her from the dressing room mirror. She was marginally, begrudgingly satisfied that her face looked about right for what it had to do. A subtle touch of razzle-dazzle. Real-hair half-lashes. Close attention to detail, right down to her silver slippers.

Carrie checked her wristwatch. If everything went well, she was about six hours away from Washington now. All she had to do was slip quietly past the police, the CIA, and half the army of San Dominica.

At 1:30 on the dot, Carrie Rose left for Robert Kennedy Airport with her fingers, legs, and eyes crossed. And when she walked into the airport terminal, she discovered that her dressing room preparation had really been quite thorough. She needn't have worried.

She looked like just about every other woman there.

By 2:30 Carrie Rose was on a Pan Am flight out of the Caribbean.

When the three o'clock news from Puerto Rico came on the brassy transistor radio nearby, Damian started to gather up his clothes. The tall blond man put on dark sunglasses, a white deckhand's hat, a white cotton-madras shirt.

At 3:10 he walked into a shabby open-air cafe. The outdoor restaurant ran the length of Cape John Beach on thin, crusty gray pilings—pelican's legs.

From the cafe pay phone, Rose called the American embassy.

Receptionist.

Male secretary.

Put on hold.

Three-seventeen.

Three twenty-one. Getting slightly humorous.

Brooks Campbell finally spoke. "Hello, this is Campbell."

Damian said, "Listen very carefully and don't say a fucking word until I'm finished. . . . In fifty-four minutes, at four-fifteen, Colonel Dred is going to commit his first major act of violence. This will be the *final* act we've planned for you. . . ."

"Rose! . . ."

"Shut the fuck up! . . . We expect you to try to stop us from leaving San Dominica after this. But if you do, I'm going to kill you. I promise you, Campbell. Here's to poor Nickie Handy, chump.''

"Rose."

Click.

"Goddammit, stop playing games!" Brooks Campbell screamed into the loud buzzing of the telephone.

Shortly after Rose's call, Campbell contacted Harold Hill in Washington.

"All hell is about to break loose here. I'm going to need a lot of help now. But I'm going to get them, Harry."

"I think you will. I really do," said Harry the Hack.

Click.

At 5:30, feeling desperate and confused, Peter Macdonald telephoned Campbell at the U.S. embassy. He was informed by a very official-sounding American man that Mr. Campbell had left for the day. Peter was then told that all Americans were being asked to stay off the streets.

There'd been a massacre.

Click.

Elizabeth's Fancy, San Dominica

Tyndall's Goat Highway goes nowhere except to a restored nineteenth-century sugar-cane plantation called Elizabeth's Fancy—and when Elizabeth's Fancy closes at four each afternoon, the Goat Highway goes nowhere.

The last bus from the plantation carried the final tour groups back to their hotels. It also brought back a woman ticket taker, a forty-two-year-old bartender-manager from Liverpool, England, and three security guards from Tanner Men.

The bus was a tongue-red-and-black double-decker manufactured by Rolls-Royce in 1953. Its nickname was Grasshopper.

Grasshopper had a maximum speed of forty-four MPH and misaligned springs that made it appear to hop down the bumpy Goat Highway. Because its second deck was so much higher than the jungle brush, Grasshopper could be seen from five miles away.

In this case, however, the red top half of the bus was being observed from just two miles off.

The three black men standing at the edge of the Goat Highway all held high-powered M-16 rifles manufactured in Detroit, Michigan. Just behind them stood a line of teenage boys. Each boy held a sharp machete knife.

"How'd you compaare dis M-16 an th' old M-14?" Colonel Dred was saying to the African.

Kingfish Toone's eyes didn't move away from the dirt road. Right beside him, the Cuban was toeing dust like a stubborn or angry horse. He was looking forward to shooting Dred very much now.

"There is no comparison." The African's deep voice finally came. "The M-16 will strike any target with three times the impact of a conventional rifle. It would shoot straight through a line of five men." The mercenary took a silver bullet out of his shirt pocket. He held the bullet lengthwise between thick, coal-black fingers.

"Still another war toy. Invented by the Americans, I suppose. The shell is coated with plastic. It leaves no stains. Impossible to find with a medical X-ray. Quite diabolical, really. Think about it, Colonel Dred."

"Dey cost?" the guerrilla asked. "Th' guns, nah dose bullet. Diabolik bullet you have."

"I don't follow costs very closely." Toone shrugged. "Perhaps five hundred apiece for the rifles."

"*Hyiuuu.*" The guerrilla chief shrieked and laughed. Then Dred walked away to make a last check on his soldiers.

In the back of his mind was the delicious thought that within hours he would be more important than Che, maybe even than Fidel Castro. Something like a black Arafat . . . holding the sun for ransom instead of oil.

The driver of the red bus, forty-nine-year-old Franklin James, was feeling sweaty and itchy and most of all malcontent, this particularly sweaty afternoon. As the antique double-decker bumped along, he could feel the whole Goat Highway in the palm of his hand. In the shivering black knob of the stick shift.

Jus' what is th' problem now? James talked to himself. Tired of drivin' dis funny-time bus. Earnin' yo' money too easy, hey, mon? What to break yo' ass for it lak nigger? Admit it, mon, yo' got it easy. Admit to yo'self, truth, Franklin. . . .

Just to break the everyday monotony, though, the driver thought he would do something revolutionary today: go left instead of right at the vee in the road about a quarter of a mile ahead. He would take the scenic route instead of the Goat Highway this day. Through the old sugar-cane fields.

Franklin James looked in his rearview mirror and saw straw beach hats and lobster red faces. A pretty blond bitch in a halter top was playing with her tittie straps. There were a few empty seats for a change, too.

At the vee in the road, the bus driver took a left instead of the usual Goat Highway route. As he made the wrong turn, the red-faced manager of Elizabeth's Fancy jumped up in the third seat of the bus.

"This is the wrong road, you idiot bastard. Back it up, boy. Get on the Goat road."

Which Franklin James did with a subservient

smile and not a word of protest. Admit it, mon, yo' got it easy.

Most of Dred's men were lying on their stomachs back twenty to forty yards from the dirt road. A few bare-chested boys had shimmied up into coconut trees.

Colonel Dred was paying no attention. Instead the twenty-seven-year-old man watched the burly African and the Cuban.

A man smoking a cigarette and wearing a striped woolen hat shouted to Dred from out of a tree. "Dey comin' 'round in 'bout annudder minute." The soldier slipped his cigarette butt down out of the tree.

Monkey Dred turned and gave a hand gesture to the rest of his guerrillas. The sound of rifles clicked off echoes on both sides of the Goat Highway.

Then Dred put the sleek M-16 to his own cheek. He sighted it very carefully.

Squeezed.

Squeezed.

The whole top half of the Cuban's head splattered. Blood splashed onto tall stalks of grass as far as thirty feet away. Kingfish Toone was thrown forward with his huge black arms stretched out wide, a big dark hole in the back of his khaki shirt.

"Bad kind a niggers," Monkey Dred shouted to the soldier in the tree. "Drivin' Cadillac. Warin' perfuume, yo' know."

Besides, the executions had been well paid for by Damian Rose. They'd earned Dred two more precious machine guns.

Speckles of red splashed through a latticework of jungle green. Then Colonel Dred could see the upper deck of the bus again. Sun rays ricocheted off the scaling red roof. Some banana wrens passed by. Every window in the old bus was flung open wide. Americans, Germans, English, and South Americans looked out on handsome mahogany trees, blooming wild lilies, parakeets.

Jungle, mahn, jungle.

"Ay pretty!" Dred shouted to the treetop birds. Jacamars. Parrots. His adrenaline was flowing like the teeming streets of Trenchtown. The juices made him feel like a Rastafarian superman. *Jah*. A walking, fast-talking contradiction.

The teetering double-decker bus had turned down a narrow straightaway less than a hundred yards away. It was coming straight at them, down a tunnel of coconut and fir trees.

Dred's men began to talk to one another. Enthusiastic shouts. Hypertense babble.

The red bus was fuzzy and just a little unreal through shimmering waves of heat. High blond weeds fanned away from it like flying hair. Palms and ferns loudly scraped the roof and windows.

Dred was staring so hard, anticipating so very

much, that the bus seemed to stop moving. To freeze on the straightaway.

"Ro-bert," he screamed. "Ro-bert!"

A tiny rifleman with sick yellow eyes and a yellow Che beret came running up beside him. The man's big M-16 rifle made him seem like a child.

"Stay by me, Robert. Now watch closely. I want you to shoot it."

As if the red bus were a charging elephant.

Up ahead, Franklin James watched a young woman and boy step into the Goat Highway. Barefoot, dressed in sun-bleached rags, they stood in the middle of the road, both of them waving excitedly at the bus.

James cursed to himself, but he touched his foot to the brakes. He shifted gears and, before the bus stopped fully, had the folding doors crashing open. "Hey, what is it, woman?" the fat black man shouted angrily.

"Yo' can take us to main road?" the woman screamed through the open bus door. "Bway is bahd sick, mon."

The bus driver's face took on a pained look. "Oh, lay-dy! I can't ride no-body not fram dat plantation, yo' know."

"My bway is sick!" the black woman screamed.

Suddenly a rifle shot crashed through the top right

corner of the bus windshield. The entire half of the windshield fell back inside the bus.

Franklin James put his foot to the ground, and the Grasshopper bucked and jumped forward.

The hollow popping sound of M-16 rifles erupted everywhere.

Not thirty yards away from Dred's men, the tall, gawky bus seemed to strike a giant pothole. The bus slid quietly to the center of the road. It seemed to ride on its right tires for a while. Then it swerved sharply to the left.

Franklin James was already dead, bumping back and forth over the steering wheel. People inside the bus were falling out of their seats.

Like an enormous lawn mower, the double-decker ran over five- and six-foot-high ferns, thick brush, small trees. It hit a huge royal palm straight on, and the palm tree tore back through the engine and cab. The tree trunk continued five feet down the aisle, crushing people in the front seats, and then the Grasshopper finally came to a stop.

Gaping holes began to mottle the side of the bus that faced into the firing squad.

On the second level of the bus, the Tanner security guards answered the rifle fire with a few pistol shots. When the guards were lucky they managed to hit somewhere in the trees, where Dred's men were systematically destroying the bus. Shooting it to bits.

The heads of dead passengers sat still in several of the open windows. The broken engine had begun to spew thick black smoke. A few of the bus passengers climbed out far-side windows, tried to run, and were shot down. A small blond boy in red shorts lay dead in the grass to one side of the bus. An older man lay beside a big, black front tire. A twelve-year-old girl ran like the horses on her father's farm—a beautiful little girl from Surrey, England—and she was a survivor.

For ten minutes there were shouts and stomach-freezing screams from the forty-odd people trapped in the bus. Then there was no sound except for the lazy popping of M-16 rifles.

Colonel Dred and his marksman, Robert, walked to the bus in smoky, devastating silence. As they got up close, parrots and jacamars began to scream in the trees again. The tiny marksman took out a dull black Liberator pistol.

The two disappeared into the bus, and more gunshots were fired. A man screamed inside the bus. Another muffled gunshot sounded inside.

When they came out again, Dred waved to the four boys standing up on the Goat Highway. Each of the four had a long, scary fright wig. Each held a shiny field machete with a red neckerchief tied around the hilt.

At the same time, the other rebel soldiers were getting up out of the brush; dropping down from the trees. The guerrillas began to light up ganja sticks, regular cigarettes, cheap cigars. Only a few of them came forward to examine the bus.

It was Dred himself who saw the beige-and-green shadow moving through the thick backwoods behind the red bus. He recognized the face of Damian Rose, a pink smudge among the trees and bright green bushes. A shiny white smile.

"Aaagghh, Rose. Jeezus, mahn!" The young guerrilla screamed as he realized what was going to happen. He tried to turn away.

The first rifle shot pierced the back of his head; it came out where the black man's nose and mouth had been. The wound was very hot, and for a split second Dred's eyes and nose seemed to be on fire. The ground rushed up at his face, and then it all disappeared on him.

He was falling down a pitch-black hole that echoed his screams—*R . . . o . . . s . . . e . . .*

By 6:00 P.M. that night, the president of the United States knew about it.

Five members of the Cabinet Committee to Combat Terrorism—the chief of staff; the assistant to the president for national security affairs; the press secretary for the president; the secretary of defense; and the director of the CIA—sat with him in the Oval Office of the White House.

The director of the CIA briefed the chief executive

on selected facts about Lathrop Wells, Nevada; the Forlenzas; Isadore Goldman; Damian and Carrie Rose; San Dominica. His primary recommendation at the moment was that the contract operators Damian and Carrie Rose be eliminated immediately. Searched out and destroyed.

"You're shitting me," the president of the United States said after he'd heard the entire story. He looked around his Oval Office. At the chief of staff. At his press secretary. At his assistant for national security. "Somebody tell me this man is shitting me. That's an order."

From 6:30 in the evening on, the world's TV and radio stations interrupted their regular programming to announce that the leftist San Dominican rebel, Colonel Dassie Dred, had been killed during an attack on a tourist bus some twenty-five miles east of the capital city of Coastown.

At 8:00 P.M. Carrie arrived in Washington, D.C. Now the tricky stuff began.

PART II

The Perfect Escape

May 8, 1979, Tuesday
Bay of
Pigs II

Chapter Nineteen

> Damian and I had violent arguments
> about the Escape. My point of view: get
> out of the Caribbean immediately.
> Damian's: finish the operation as it should
> be finished. Take care of Campbell and
> Harold Hill right. Stop them from coming
> after us. . . . That was how Macdonald
> became important. Also how Damian got
> the idea for what happened in
> Washington.
>
> The Rose Diary

May 8, 1979; Fairfax Station, Virginia

Tuesday Morning. The Eighth Day of the Season.

The morning after the massacre at Elizabeth's Fancy, Mark Hill took a fast shower, combed his thick blond hair, then put on a freshly washed Washington Redskins sweatshirt and neat bell-bottom jeans.

The handsome teenager looked in the mirror over his bureau and gave himself an "okay" sign and a broad, comical wink.

Downstairs, he could hear his mother busily making breakfast. Fried-bacon smells were drifting upstairs. Bacon, and also fresh coffee, which Mark hated with a sincere passion.

The fourteen-year-old quickly brushed his teeth and used the family Water Pik. Then he took the front stairs in three broad jumps. He strode casually into the kitchen, unconsciously imitating a pro football quarterback named Bill Kilmer.

Bright sunshine streamed through the open back door and the saffron-curtained window over the sink. A man and a woman in white terrorist masks stood in front of the sink, on either side of his mother. Each of the two held a long-barreled black revolver.

"You just listen to what these people say." Carole Hill spoke in a calm voice that made the boy wonder how his mother had gotten so brave so quickly.

Carrie Rose watched the boy through narrow eye slits in her mask. "That's right, Mark. We're not here to hurt either of you. Sit down there at the table. Your mother will make you some breakfast."

Never once taking his eyes off the intruders, the teenager slowly sat down.

Carole Hill walked over to her stove slowly and cautiously. Her hands trembled as she started to turn her bacon with a table fork. Little spits of grease flew up at her apron and face. "My husband will be home soon," she said matter-of-factly. "He just—"

Carrie smiled under her mask. "Carole Ann, your husband isn't even in the country right now. Relax. Cook us all a nice breakfast, okay? We're going to be spending the day together, it looks like."

The man with her, a New York gunman by the name of Kruger, sat down across from Mark at the breakfast table. "Pay it no mind," the man said. "Doesn't concern you, Mark."

"How do you know my name?" was the boy's first question.

"Oh, we're friends of your father's." Carrie smiled.

CHAPTER TWENTY

One girl's candid evaluation of the CIA's
Caribbean Account in '75. . . . Basic
ineptitude down to a formal science. An
inordinate paranoia about Fidel Castro,
and/or Moscow. Paranoia about potential
trouble in Puerto Rico. Paranoia over
Cuban troops in Africa. A gross
overestimation of Dassie Dred. A correct
evaluation of Joseph Walthey as a
potential strongman pig and ally. . . .
Mostly bad information of all things. Bad
Intelligence. . . .

The Rose Diary

Coastown, San Dominica

That same morning in Coastown, forty-four-year-
old Harold Hill yawned so that his jaw cracked.
He stretched his thin arms and made eating noises

with his lips, teeth, sticky furred tongue. He took off his horn-rimmed glasses and massaged the bridge of his nose.

Harold Hill then rearranged himself on a sighing wing chair inside the U.S. embassy.

He glanced through an army report on Peter Macdonald: "Peter Stillwell Macdonald. Born Grand Rapids, Michigan; 1950. Son of a U.S. Army colonel and a high school mathematics teacher. Youngest of six sons. U.S.M.A. 1969–71. Honorable Discharge. Above-average intelligence. Inferiority complex caused in part by older brothers' successes. . . . Mixes well but prefers to stay alone. . . . No close friends. . . . Subject of homosexual probe ('73—all branches): negative. . . . Strong combat skills but ambivalent attitude about current war. A model top sergeant. . . ."

Tossing aside that report, Hill looked back at a yellow legal pad where he'd been free-associating about the Roses. He looked at a black folder marked "Secret—Sensitive." Then back at the legal pad. It was 5:00 A.M., and Hill hadn't slept since six the previous morning.

At the top of the yellow, blue-lined sheet, "Carrie & Damian Rose" was centered and underlined in red. The rest of the paper was covered with neat black handwriting in orderly columns. Ideas, phrases, names, reminders . . . fourteen items.

1. Tall. Blond. English-looking. Has shopped at Harrods.

2. St. Louis Hotel in Paris . . . Nickie Handy shot by woman in nearby bistro. Carrie? . . . Handy used by Campbell (1972). Coincidence?

3. Carrie: fair-haired; supposed to be a stunner; tall . . . beware! Don't be a chauvinist, shithead! Carrie is as dangerous as Damian.

4. Husband and wife squabbles . . . absolutely. . . . So What?

5. Dr. Meral Johnson. Street-smart. Useful? How best?

6. Peter Macdonald should be found today. Cajoled. Useful!!!!

7. Marines from South America. Colonel Fescoe. Hindrance!!

8. Prop planes going out at night. Marijuana to New Orleans. Shoot down? Shoot down.

9. Coast Guard can blockade island effectively. . . . Search private craft especially. . . . Would Goldman help Roses escape? Think so. . . .

10. Can't let Joseph Walthey go crazy executing Dred's people. This is important.*****

11. Why Damian Rose phone calls to Campbell? Important!

12. Clue in their organized disorganization also. Important! . . . Stu Leedman coming from L.A. . . . Czech: killing team on Rose's level on loan from Interpol. Hindrance!!

13. Lucky 13! Damian probably a psycho.

14. Pattern suggests bigger plays to come. Anti-pattern suggests no further plays. . . . Operative word is "play." Have to learn to "play," or lose this one in grand style.********

Harold Hill got up and paced around the large oak-and-brass embassy office. VIP office: like presidential suite at famous hotels. Private bath, breakfast nook. The nuts!

There was no way the Roses were going to get off San Dominica, he considered.

No, there was a way, plenty of ways—but Hill was trying to convince himself that Damian Rose had programmed himself to make a mistake before he took one of them. . . . The telephone calls to Brooks Campbell. Those were the key. Crank calls!

Harold Hill didn't have very much to go on—but he did have something: Damian Rose was a tall, blond, English-looking megalomaniac. With luck he could be had.

Hill finally put his cream suit jacket over his arm and walked out of the big, cool embassy mansion. He believed that he'd made a beginning, at least. A good night's work.

A big red sun was just coming over the green hills that rose high over the perfect little city and the sea. It was a loud sun that would eventually give Hill a headache that day.

Two badly trained soldiers stood out by the front gates, laughing and poking at each other. They reminded Hill how little the people of these countries ever got involved in the realities of their situation.

As he passed by the soldiers, Hill tipped his Panama hat and smiled. As he did so, he automatically thought of the famous poster mocking Richard Nixon. *Why is this man smiling?* the poster read. Why indeed?

CHAPTER TWENTY-ONE

If everything went as Damian expected it
to, we were to meet at the Hilton Hotel in
Morocco on or around May 12. If not, not.
The Rose Diary

Cap Foyle, San Dominica

At a quarter past five on May 8, an old James
Taylor song was blasting in Peter's head—"Sweet
Baby James." He was also being mesmerized by
the sight of twenty black soldiers guarding the remains of the bus from Elizabeth's Fancy.

The young American watched the quiet, terrible
scene for ten or fifteen minutes, planted it forever
in his war atrocities file, then left to forage around
for something to eat.

For some disconnected reason, he had the Super
Six on his mind: Neddy, Huey, Deli Bob, Bernie,

Tailspin Tommy. And little Pete—Little Mac. As he rode away from the ambushed bus, Peter couldn't help thinking that in his humble opinion, he was way, way out of his league right now. Even in Special Forces they didn't prepare you for this kind of miserable shit.

At about that same time, Damian Rose pinched a blue mite off the sleeve of a pale sand overshirt.

At 5:30 A.M. he stood tall and wide awake inside a phone booth in the neolithic farming village of Cap Foyle. Rose asked for number twenty-six and waited for his connection.

Two sleepy Cap Foyle residents, an old man and a girl, were already pushing skeletal bicycles along the town's dusty streets. Two cross streets down from them was the sharp green Caribbean.

"Hello . . . I say hello—"

Damian cut off Brooks Campbell by shouting at the sleepy-sounding man—screaming at the top of his lungs into the telephone. *"You only have eight hours, asshole!* Eight hours to decide to stop chasing us. To live up to your side of the contract. . . . If you're looking for us by midnight tonight, I guarantee both you and Hill will be sorrier than you can dream. I guarantee it! You have until midnight to be intelligent for once in your pitiful little grease-stain lives."

Damian then hung up the phone. The tall blond man walked back to his car, humming a favorite tune—"Lili Marlene." He was beginning to enjoy his escape plan.

Meanwhile, twelve rather striking-looking men were making their separate ways to San Dominica. They were coming from Miami and New York. From Acapulco, Caracas, San Juan. Each of the twelve was an expensive male model. From the Ford Agency. From Wilhelmina Men. From Stewart and Zoli.

They'd all been hired by Carrie the week before. To pose for brochures for the new Le Pirat Hotel and for the Dragon Reef Condominium Homes. They'd been specially selected off composite and head sheets at rates of $500 plus expenses per day.

The peculiar thing was that all twelve men were between six feet two and six feet four.

All were strikingly blond.

All looked terribly, terribly English.

Part two of the curious adventure had begun. The perfect escape.

CHAPTER TWENTY-TWO

Casinos are now being built by all the big
motels. The island will have one bad
season. Maybe two. Maybe even three. But
then it will boom like nothing even they
can imagine. The island has four times the
area of Nassau and New Providence. It's
twice as beautiful as Jamaica. It should
become Monte-Carlo West.

The Rose Diary

These days it is fashionable to be against
the Americans. It is my hope to be in the
vanguard of a countermovement, which, I
suspect, could be equally fashionable one
day. That is—to be for the Americans.

Joseph Walthey

Coastown, San Dominica

Tuesday Afternoon.

While all this was going on, Brooks Campbell sat hunched over a steaming pot of very strong, very good Blue Mountain coffee from Jamaica. During the morning and early afternoon of May 8, the young CIA man made person-to-person, heart-to-heart telephone calls to some of the best homicide men in the world.

In the big office next door, Harold Hill was doing much the same thing on a slightly larger scale.

Calls went out to Mr. Alexander Somerset, the commissioner of crime at Scotland Yard; to Edward Mahoney in the Office of Domestic Intelligence in Washington; to the Assassination Bureau in Paris. Calls went to the biggest crime men in West Germany, Italy, Spain, Canada. . . .

The subject was top priority and very confidential, the conversations made clear:

"A very large, very private manhunt is now being conducted throughout the Caribbean and South America. The objects of the hunt are two slithery white soldiers of fortune who have taught a ragtag band of guerrillas how to fight and think like Mau-Maus, the PLO, and the Japanese army. Who have, among other things, massacred forty-nine civilians on board a bus. The names are Damian and Carrie Rose.''

The slip-catch was that the United States was handling the search like a top-secret, national security matter. The clear implication: Somebody had goofed again in the Caribbean.

The exact nature of the mistake remained a secret. A top secret.

Before it was over, though, some wisenheimer at Interpol had nicknamed the operation Bay of Pigs II. By Sunday that slogan was a headline in London's *Observer*.

Beginning unofficially at 6:00 P.M. on May 8, officially at 9:00 A.M. on the ninth, a straight-faced, very serious attempt was made to take the eighty-one-by-thirty-nine-mile island of San Dominica, turn it upside down, and shake, shake, shake it like a child's piggy bank.

The long-shot hope was that both Roses and Peter Macdonald would tumble out into the waiting arms of Brooks Campbell and Harold Hill.

Beginning at nine, government sound trucks began to rumble through major cities and the surrounding countryside. These trucks broadcast the politest lilting-voiced descriptions of a tall, blond, English-looking man; of a young American man, Peter Macdonald.

Meanwhile CCF soldiers and U.S. Marines from

Georgia and Florida searched the beaches, the grasslands, even the island's large, steamy rain forest: West Hills. An exhaustive house-by-house, hotel-by-hotel search was begun in the cities of Coastown, Port Gerry, and Cape John.

Also, every country represented on the Elizabeth's Fancy bus sent some kind of special help: Germany; the United States; England; Canada; France; Israel; Trinidad; Jamaica; Argentina; Texas. Ballistics, riot, and interrogation experts were hurried in from New York and Washington. More federal marshals were flown in to help keep order in the cities. Headhunters, including a special team called "Czech"—came from as far away as Eastern Europe. Bounties totaling more than $150,000 were set.

Learning that "an English-looking man" was being sought, a small group was set up at Interpol's Secretariat in St. Cloud, France. Information on known gunrunners and mercenaries was collated and sent out from Interpol's Criminal Records Department. Extensive checks were made on the dead men, Kingfish Toone and the Cuban, Blinkie Tomas.

Through all of this, Campbell and Harold Hill's "lead" on the Roses was never once questioned. Even the bitterest of police-world cynics wouldn't speculate and couldn't come up with what had actually happened in the Caribbean.

By early night of the first day, the hunt had turned up eight tall blond men. Two-thirds of the twelve.

Looking in on the eight—all blond, all handsome as hell, all between six feet two and six feet four—Federal Marshal Stuart Leedman of Los Angeles got the feeling that somebody wasn't telling him everything he needed to know about this grisly case. Something was as fishy as San Diego Sea World, Stu Leedman was thinking.

"Now what do you do for a living?" he asked Antoine Coffey, a wispy blond who had listed his address as the World of Free Spirits.

The blond model seemed confused by the question. "A living?"

"Yeah," Stu Leedman said. "What do you do for money, Antoine? How do you pay the rent? Get money to go to the movies?"

Coffey smiled suddenly. "Oh, *that*," he whispered. "Thhodomy, you mean."

Marshal Stuart Leedman stood up in the quiet examination room and screamed at the open door.

"Who ordered in all these blond faggots?" His voice carried up and down the serene, dignified hallway of the U.S. embassy. "What the *fuck*, *Jesus Christ*, *shit* is going on around this pisshole?"

It was every bit as maddening and confusing as the machete murders themselves. More so, because it came on top of them . . . which was exactly the way Damian wanted it.

Port Gerry, San Dominica

Tuesday Evening.

His nose pressed against the cool green glass of the number 9 bus window, Peter watched a row of flowered shirts drift by on Station Street. Stranger in Paradise, he thought.

He saw pink-and-purple shirts like the Spanish in big cities always wore. Leather mushroom caps and tiny fedoras. Black wraparound sunglasses. San Dominican country boys trying to look like the Tonton Macoutes.

People seemed to be forever waiting for buses around San Dominica, Peter had begun to notice. The Elizabeth's Fancy bus massacre was mind-blowing when you thought about it like that. It was like attacking an interstate highway in the United States. Severing a main artery.

Black women in homemade dresses and sandals were pressed up closer to the station. A nest of young conchie girls. "Queen bees," they called them around Coastown.

As the number 9 bus started to brake, Macdonald put his hand on the Colt .44 under his shirt. His heart started to thump. . . . Peter had begun to imagine the tall blond man waiting around every corner, behind every palm tree. Like some slick, handsome bogeyman. Waiting just for him. . . .

The bus station was a wooden shack covered with antique beer and Coke signs worth more than the building itself. Stopping in front, the number 9 bucked and shivered like an old belly dancer. All the people and livestock being transported inside woke up suddenly. Chickens squawked and flapped red-and-white wings like fans. A goat started kicking the seats, and an old black man started kicking the goat.

"Ay maum in dat blue dress!" a Rude Boy shouted out a bus window.

There was a loud *whoosh*ing of steaming hot air, and the driver said something Macdonald couldn't follow. People started walking off the bus, though, and Peter guessed that he was there.

This hole-in-the-wall must be the summer capital of Port Gerry.

Eating a thirty-cent meat pie from the station canteen, Peter climbed a dark street with no sidewalks. With dreary two- and three-story limestone buildings on either side.

The pie smelled like bad breath, the street smelled like human sweat. Peter's body felt as if it would collapse pretty soon. . . . The last time he remembered feeling so bad was when he'd had dysentery in Thailand.

He was feeling lonely as hell, too. Thought about Jane constantly.

The first time he'd seen her at the Plantation Inn,

he'd thought she was trouble. Quiet—only with a bad dose of New York city smug . . . quick wise-ass front. Shooting down every guy who said hello to her at the inn. In Peter's mind she was a blond version of Ali MacGraw. Trouble. . . . One weekend, though, he'd asked her if she wanted to go on a cross-island trip with him. See the West Hills' jungle. See the beaches on the other side. And surprise! She'd said sure. . . . Twenty-four hours later the two of them still hadn't stopped talking. An amazing day of straight talk about each other. Striking chords in each other like crazy. Strangers, practically. Crying together before the first day was over. Huddled together on a dark, deserted beach called Runaway . . . because they'd both been so damn lonely. Because there'd been so many things they'd wanted to tell somebody. . . .

Halfway up the hill, Peter saw a sign: RENT. Another sign: ROOMS; it showed a little black angel sleeping on folded hands.

A doorway at the crest of the hill read WELCOME, and that seemed just about right to Peter.

A tall goateed man and a boy sat at a buckling table covered with dominoes, in the foyer.

"Yes, mon?" The older fellow spoke. A soft, serious voice, much more businesslike than Peter expected from the look of the place from outside.

"I need a room, please. I'm very tired."

The black man looked at Peter strangely.

Shrugged. Then he went to a little school desk, where he scrawled a line in a red ledger. He took six dollars in advance for the room.

"Dis bway will take yo' up. Yo' be served breakfas' in de mornin', mon."

The young boy pointed to a dark stairway. Then he walked ahead of Macdonald, holding a candle in a soup dish.

The boy began to whisper to Peter as they climbed the stairs. His small candle slowly revealed the hotel, like in a murder mystery.

"T'marra yo' cum fishin' in me fadder boat, mon. Catch grouper. Lotsa big snappers, too."

Peter suddenly started to laugh when they reached the top of the stairs. "I'm sorry." He turned to the boy. "I'm not laughing at you. I can't go fishing tomorrow, though."

"Too bad, mon. Yo' missin' good shit."

Peter and the black boy turned into a slanting, lopsided hallway with unpainted doors on both sides of a long, tattered runner. A dim light shone at the other end of the hall. A black telephone sat on the floor under the light. Suddenly Peter understood that this was an all-black hotel. Welcome.

Inside his room, he hid his wallet between the rusty pipes of the sink. He bumped his head hard on the pipes and felt strangely, ridiculously exhilarated. For a minute he even forgot about the tall blond man. The butcher.

Then he just sat on the bed with his head propped up so he faced the door. With the Colt revolver lying across his boxer shorts. Listening to the ricky-tick rhythms of reggae out in the streets; listening to pigs rooting in the hotel's backyard.

Before he could sleep, he had the urge to go back out into the moldy hallway. He picked up the black telephone and asked for number 107. He got through to a night operator with a beautiful lilting voice. Nightbird. Then to a groggy, very distant-sounding woman. Then to Jane.

"Hiya, Laurel." Peter's face lit up with a sleepy smile. "This is Oliver Hardy speaking. I think I'm going crazy, babe. . . ."

CHAPTER TWENTY-THREE

Our strategy for Brooks Campbell was a
simple one: we tried to give him too many
choices and produce decision stress.
Harold Hill was a completely different
problem. We went right for Hill's balls.

The Rose Diary

Fairfax Station, Virginia

At 2:30 in the morning, two Virginia state troopers, James Walsh and Dominick Niccolo, tramped
across the dewy back lawns of a big white house
way out in the sticks.

A nearby neighbor had reported that something
strange was going on at the house. What sounded
like screams for help.

Around at the back, the policemen discovered
that the kitchen door wasn't locked. Not all that

unusual for the rural community of Fairfax Station. Not usual, though.

Inside the kitchen they were greeted with the loud ticking of an electric clock. The hum of a refrigerator. The indistinct sounds of an empty, or sleeping, house.

The kitchen was lit by an orangish night-light over the sink. Several coffee cups and half a box of Dunkin' Donuts were sitting on the kitchen table. The remains of half a dozen sandwiches.

Dom Niccolo turned on the hall light and called out in a high-pitched tenor's voice. "Hello. Is anyone home? This is the Virginia State Police."

No answer.

The two men continued to walk through the dark house, turning on lights. Calling out, "Is anyone home?"

A standard lamp in the living room was already on. As they entered the comfortably furnished room, they were startled by the loud crashing of the refrigerator making ice.

"That son of a bitch." James Walsh grit his teeth.

The troopers heard another noise. A young black retriever came running downstairs, wagging its tail and jumping up on the two men, licking them.

"Pup scared the shit out of me, too." Walsh grinned.

"Jesus Christ, Jimmy." Dom Niccolo knelt to

look closer at the dog. "She has blood all over her side. Look at this, Jimmy."

Both men unholstered their sidearms.

"This is the Virginia State Police!" Niccolo called from the foot of the stairs.

"We better get some more help here," Walsh whispered.

Niccolo motioned for him to shut up. "Come on."

Dominick Niccolo, then James Walsh, headed up the shag-carpeted stairway. Both men had their guns pointed up into the dark hallway above.

Right at the top of the stairs they found a woman.

Carole Hill was barefoot, dressed in a flowered blouse and white walking shorts. Blood was caked on her face and chest. A pool of blood was on the carpet beside her.

Two bedrooms down the hall, James Walsh found a teenage boy.

Mark Hill was inside his clothes closet. The boy was gagged and tied up with a telephone wire. But at least he was alive.

In the master bedroom, Dominick Niccolo was calling the trooper barracks in Alexandria. "The house is on Shad Stream Road," he said into a pink princess telephone. "Belongs to Mr. and Mrs. Harold Hill. The husband doesn't seem to be here. . . . Johnny, you won't believe this, but there's a three-foot machete stuck in the poor woman's heart. Jimmy Walsh is up here puking in the hallway. Hurry up, will you? . . .''

The machete murders had come to America. Almost to Langley. Just fourteen miles from the White House.

The warning couldn't have been any clearer.

May 9, 1979,
Wednesday
Stalk
Tall
Blond
Man

CHAPTER TWENTY-FOUR

From the Rose Diary

In December of 1978 I had wired, then telephoned, our last important player—an expensive English shooter named Clive Lawson. At that time, Lawson was buying and selling cocaine and four-star pornography in North Miami Beach, Florida.

During our eventual phone conversation, I told Lawson that Señor Miguel Alvarez of Caracas (Pietra Forte) and Anthony Patriarca of Miami (Cosa Nostra) were my sponsors; that I was interested in purchasing a large stock of 16-millimeter films I heard he had, or could get.

"Do you have anything that might stimulate older gentlemen?" I asked him over the phone. "Large, private screenings for older gentlemen?"

Lawson said that he might have something. He didn't know. He didn't do business over the phone.

On the fifteenth of December, we met in the very unlikely Poodle Bar at the Fontainebleau Hotel.

For our meeting, the English killer was wearing a wrinkled white shirt. A funky plaid sports jacket. Thick, black-rimmed glasses that were so square-looking, I couldn't quite believe them. . . . Because, you see, Clive Lawson was an exceptionally handsome man. A little like Michael Caine from a distance. A lot like Damian.

He ordered Tanqueray with a twist, and I had something chic like Campari. Both of us played our parts for a while, then I simply announced to him that I was Carrie Rose.

After that admission, we talked about the Congo and Southeast Asia—places where we'd both worked and vaguely heard of each other. We talked about how Clive had fallen into the pornography business through the Pietra Forte—the so-called Latin-American Connection. We talked about Damian and me.

Then, as factually yet vaguely as possible, I explained something about San Dominica to the English killer.

"As a further introduction," I said at the end of my opening gambit, "I have to tell you that we can't let anyone in on the total picture down there. Like who holds the contract. That's rule number one. . . . On the other hand, we're offering very large fees for peripheral work that shouldn't be all that hard.''

The green eyes behind Lawson's black-rimmed glasses sparkled like large emeralds. He had a relaxed, confident manner that I was beginning to like. ''My favorite sort of work,'' he said. ''Do go on.''

''For one week in May,'' I continued, ''your job will be to lead the San Dominican police on a wild-goose chase all over the island. That's where your time in the Congo fits in nicely for our purposes. It's also where you earn your money.''

Lawson's eyebrows arched a little. ''Will I be shooting at people? Or getting shot at?''

''If you're careless, you'll get shot at, I'm sure. The usual ground rules apply, Clive. There will be at least two hits for you. Probably military targets. Lower-echelon assholes.''

The tall blond man smiled. He understood perfectly. At least he thought he understood: he was to run cover for our escape.

''How much?'' he asked next.

''Fifty thousand dollars.''

Lawson started to laugh. ''No haggling, ay? I don't even get a chance to try and bargain you up. All right, I think so. . . . How about sixty? I assume I have to get my own behind out of there. . . .''

''Sixty is fine.''

''Money in advance, of course.''

"Of course."

I laid it right out in front of the English killer. A fat brown envelope on the Fontainebleau bar.

Damian and I had just purchased one of the most expensive pigeons in the history of crime. One of the keys to our getting away with murder.

On the morning of May 8, 1979—Tuesday—we let our pigeon fly. We had Clive Lawson make a big kill, while impersonating Damian.

CHAPTER TWENTY-FIVE

Behind every successful woman, there's a
big prick.

The Rose Diary

May 9, 1979; Coastown, San Dominica

Wednesday Morning. The Ninth Day of the Season.

Harold Hill hadn't slept well the night of the
eighth.

At 5:30 in the morning he called Brooks Campbell's home in Coastown. Yet another bizarre phone
call for poor Campbell.

"We have to get that kid Macdonald," Hill
blurted out with no introduction whatsoever—as if
he and Campbell had been carrying on the conversation all night. "For all we know now, we could
have Damian Rose locked up already. We can't
identify him by ourselves."

Brooks Campbell tried to wake himself up in a hurry. Hill was saying something that sounded important. Hill was saying something. . . .

"We, uhh . . . need someone who knows what Rose looks like," Campbell finally managed.

"Exactly," Harold Hill said. "So let's concentrate on Macdonald as much as we can today."

The configurations changed a little at 8:00 A.M. At eight Langley reached Hill with the news about his wife.

Langley didn't understand, though. Carole Hill's murder didn't make any sense.

Harry the Hack understood. Either he got Damian Rose, or Damian Rose would get him.

Port Gerry, San Dominica

That morning Peter woke with the bright Caribbean sun streaming in two windows, exploding on a mirror nailed over the sink.

A doctorbird stood on one of the windowsills, pecking at wood splinters. . . . The velvet, skull-capped head eyed the sleepy-faced man coldly, sneezed, then resumed its noisy woodworking.

"Hey. Be sociable or beat it," Peter said to the bird. He was feeling better—okay, human, anyway. Something about the hotel room, all the sunlight probably, the nearby water, reminded him of his family's place up on Lake Michigan.

In daylight the hotel was both pleasant and pleasantly ridiculous. There were different patterns of tacky wallpaper on three of the four walls, but he could also see a wide lane of cherry blue sea without getting out of bed.

"God, throw me a crumb," Peter whispered to the open window.

Sitting yogi style on the rumpled gray sheets, the ex–West Point man in him wrote out a formal battle plan on the back of a single postcard he found in the nightstand.

Rockefeller resort (Caneel Bay).
Fly Martinique? St. Thomas?
New York City . . . transfer to Washington.
Senator Pflanzer. State Department? Washington Post?
Janie flight out.
Fish 'n Fool.

The Great Escape . . . the pretty good escape, anyway.

There was a sharp rap at the hotel room door, and Peter's stomach did a dramatic elevator-shaft drop. He grabbed the Colt .44 under his bedsheets.

A pretty brown girl with a full breakfast tray peeked into the room. "Breakfus, sir."

"Oh, man." Peter moaned. "I just woke up about thirty seconds ago." He tried to smile. "It's okay. C'mon."

The girl had brought white toast with no crust. Enough marmalade and guava jelly for several loaves of bread. Steaming coffee in a child's thermos that showed cartoon pigs and a leering wolf.

Peter could see the tips of the girl's breasts as she put down the food. Pretty swaying breasts. Pretty brown legs. A nice, maidenish bum.

The girl's thin brown hands moved smoothly on the plastic dishes.

Watching her work, Peter realized that he hadn't really spoken to anyone in a day and a half—not in person, anyway. *Hi, there,* he heard several times in his mind. *I'm feeling a little nuts right now. Sit down. Have some of your good coffee there. . . .*

Peter said nothing, though. He watched the girl walk back across the room. A truly lovely little ass, heartbreaking smile—travel poster material.

"Your breakfus gettin' cold." She smiled at the door. Then she left. Peter chewed his toast and watched the songbird, unexpectedly hard and alive.

And a little more afraid because of it.

Shortly after eleven he changed into a secondhand muslin workshirt; brown chinos; a floppy blue hat.

It was a working disguise he hoped would work just one more time for him.

At quarter past he left the tiny hotel—the Welcome. Off to find a boat called the *Fish 'n Fool*.

Peter knew that the boat regularly brought guests back and forth from the expensive Rockefeller resort at Caneel Bay. From Caneel Bay he could take a prop plane to another island with safe flight connections to New York and Washington. Once he was in Washington . . . well, at least he wouldn't be in San Dominica. Someone was going to listen to him and Jane in Washington. His father had an old friend, for one thing—Senator Pflanzer. Peter himself knew an army general at the Pentagon. . . .

It was going to be weird when it hit the fan in America, Peter started to think. It was going to be devastating, in fact.

Whoever hired the blond mercenary at Turtle Bay was in for a hell of a big surprise.

Around 12:15 Peter was floating on an adrenaline high.

It was close to the feeling he'd always gotten on afternoon patrols in Asia. No-man's-'Nam. Where he'd invented new ways to block out as much shit as possible. To drift. Go with the flow.

All the world a little grainy, he was concentrating hard on a handsome black dude collecting stubs at the stern of the *Fish 'n Fool*. The dude was wearing a shocking-pink T-shirt; short-shorts; tightly wound coral bracelets and a necklace. He didn't look as if he would be any trouble, but Peter braced himself anyway.

"Parlez-vous français?" He grinned big baby-grand piano teeth at Peter. "Nope. You're American, right?"

"New York City. West Sixty-third Street." Peter lied so automatically, acted so well, it scared him a little. "We leave around twelve-thirty?"

"Twelve-thirty on the button." The young black kept his smile like a good trouser crease. "Give or take five minutes or a half hour for some of my lost *turista* friends . . . John Sampson, Norfawk, Virginah." The man put out his hand. He widened his smile. "At your beck and call, New York."

Peter finally smiled back at the man. A pseudofag! Jesus. He tilted his floppy hat down and walked up on the main deck.

The afterdeck of the *Fish 'n Fool* was all polished brass and rich mahogany. It was jam-packed with bronze gods and goddesses. With designer-signed T-shirts and Parisian jeans; forty-dollar sunglasses; the smell of benzocaine, camphor, hot burning flesh.

"Hi." Long black hair, jet-set tan. A red string bikini.

"How are you?" Peter smiled. Felt like a boat's chaplain.

"Hyellow!" Frizzy, short blond hair. Mirror sunglasses. A man.

"Hyellow."

Seeming bashful and cutely backward, Macdonald made his way to a padded bench half in, half out of the sun. He was a little self-conscious about his hair—shaggy for him; about the inescapable fact that he smelled after his days on the road.

He put his tennis sneakers up on the brass rail. Pulled the floppy hat down over his eyes. Listened to the quick beat of his good, strong heart.

Tomorrow's going to be so unreal, he thought. Washington. No idea exactly where he would start.

Then, very slowly, Peter drifted far, far away from it all. To a pretty, half-awake place with no guns, no machetes, no slick blond killers. Just Janie. Rest. Escape.

In the meantime the black dude, John Sampson, from Norfolk, Virginia, was up on shore making a phone call.

At 1:15 the sky was a roaring firefight. Flame throwers. An entire South Vietnamese city on fire.

The hat was still over his face, but Peter's eyes were open wide. He was trying to see through the loose weave of the summer fabric.

For a long moment it was almost as if he were inside a large, packed, American sports arena. A low crowd murmur echoed all around him. As if he were sitting in the bleachers during a brief lull in a dramatic World Series game. Tiger Stadium. Mickey Lolich on the mound. Everything but the hot-dog men. . . .

"Mr. Macdonald."

Crowd murmur.

"Good afternoon, Peter."

Crowd murmur.

Clammy and dry tongued, with a disgustingly sour taste in his mouth, Peter slid back the hat. He wasn't properly prepared to believe the things he saw in the blinding sunlight.

A crowd, largely blacks, was being held back on the dock by CDS soldiers. Fifty people, maybe a hundred, were all straining to watch the *Fish 'n Fool*. Policemen carrying old-fashioned rifles were running single file onto the yacht.

Close up, Macdonald tried to focus on John Sampson from Norfolk, Virginia. Then on the island police chief.

On a gray-haired American man he didn't recognize. Finally, on Brooks Campbell. White linen suit. Horn-rimmed sunglasses that were too big for him. Handsome as ever. . . .

Suddenly Peter was very tired, unbelievably weary. His head began to swim; his heart beat so hard and fast, it scared the living shit out of him.

"Good afternoon," Campbell repeated.

"You have to come with us," the black police chief said. "There's nothing to worry about."

Now there was a Bob Hope one-liner that should have gotten a laugh, Peter thought. Instead he just blinked at the four men. His mind reeled like three windows in a slot machine . . . Blond Englishmen, Colonel Dred, Cosa Nostra. Not going to get to Washington, Senator Pflanzer . . .

"Give you a hand, Macdonald."

Grubby, light bearded, he got up by himself.

All the jet-setters on the deck were standing around watching now. Whispering in one another's ears how they'd thought he looked funny when he came on board.

Tourists were aiming fancy cameras into Peter's face. Stupid, grinning bastards. Grinning soldiers with dull black rifles—phony guns that looked as if they had been carved out of soap.

Campbell and the other American man walked right beside him. A very official-looking march. Leading him through the tunnel of ambulance chasers. The other man trying to introduce himself and saying something about Hill, trying to shake Peter's hand.

Then, in the middle of the mad crowd, in the middle of everything, the police chief suddenly swung Peter around. The sweating, heavyset black man stared him right in the face, looked pained and sensitive and a little crazy himself.

"Strange, unaccountable things are still happening on our island," Meral Johnson said to Peter. The man seemed to pause out of confusion, then tears started down the rolls of his cheeks.

"Jane Cooke was killed this morning," Johnson whispered to Peter. "I'm very sorry, mister."

Mandeville, San Dominica

At quarter to ten that morning, two short-haired men in conservative gray suits had taken Jane—in a wheelchair—out a rear-door exit in the Mandeville Hospital.

As the chair whistled along a flowery path with royal palms and plumbago everywhere, the pretty blond girl was starting to smile again. Laughing for the first time in years, it seemed.

"Reminds me of Bermuda a little," one of the men said.

"Reminds me a little of *Ironsides*," Jane mumbled, a small joke.

The man pushing her wheelchair laughed through his nose. He was James McGuire, fifty-nine, a paunchy, good-natured sort who reminded Jane of Santa Claus with no white beard.

The second man, James Dowd, was just thirty-one. James Dowd was quieter than McGuire, but very nice. Very old-world Irish.

When the wheelchair was out of sight of Mandeville Hospital, deep in rich green brush, James McGuire stopped pushing.

"Okay, Janie." The red-faced man grinned. "You want to walk, you most surely can walk. You don't want to ride. I sure as heck don't want to push."

As the three Americans continued down the path, walking, they began to see more and more colorful birds, and lizards, tree frogs, hermit crabs. An ornery little mongoose was looking for a snake in the grass.

Then the winding path they were on ended abruptly in a flat, breezy field.

Jane, even the two FBI inspectors, let out short gasps of delight and awe. Beyond the field was nothing but shining, royal blue sea.

"You know, I don't think I could be anything but happy in a beautiful place like this." James Dowd finally entered the chitchatting. "I know that isn't strictly logical."

"That's how you're going to get trapped into staying here." Jane smiled at the shy, likable man. "You'll quit your job and . . . James!"

Without a sound of warning, three men suddenly appeared from behind thick brush and rocks. They wore green windbreakers and sports shirts buttoned to the throat.

"Freeze!" one of them screamed.

At the same time another man started to fire an Uzi submachine gun. A tall blond man.

Both Dowd and McGuire fell backward into high grass. Then two of the men jumped on Jane. One held down her flailing arms; the other pressed a wet handkerchief over her nose, mouth, across strands of her long, curly hair.

Understanding that it was all going to happen again, feeling as if she were on the edge of madness, Jane began to let loose amazing screams she wouldn't have believed possible.

They were putting the dripping cloth all over her face, and she was trying to bite the hand holding it. They were pushing her head back hard into the ground. Finally her arm snapped under a man's heavy leg.

Then everything was the suffocating white cloth. Its acrid, choking smell. Like trying to breathe inside a bottle of glue.

She started to give in to it finally. Blue sky, sun, angry or frightened faces flashing over her. The blond Englishman. Here. . . . She thought of Peter. Started to cry. Felt like a helpless child under their arms, legs, stomachs . . .

Then Jane bit down hard into a man's ugly, bulbous thumb.

"Don't fight. Jesus Christ," one of the men was yelling at her.

"Christ. She's biting my fucking hand!" the second man screamed.

Hospital people—white-coated doctors, nurses —finally appeared on the far side of the field.

Which is when Clive Lawson bent down and shot the struggling young woman in the right temple.

Jane thought it was the tall blond man who bent over her. Not quite as good-looking as she'd thought . . . she wanted to hold Peter just one more time. Then it all seemed so stupid and awful. . . . Then it was nothing at all.

May 10, 1979, Thursday
Dragnet
Tight.
Thousands
Stopped.

CHAPTER TWENTY-SIX

The part I was supposed to play around
Washington and Europe from the sixth to
the ninth was no part, really. It was all the
things I thought I wanted to become. . . . .
Sitting in the Gralyn Hotel. Watching a
college boy eat a sandwich outside.
Thinking that Port-Smithe is nearly
perfect. Thinking about the Loner from
Coastown. About Nickie Handy. Damian
. . . Bizarre thoughts. Like whether I'll be
alive one year from this exact
moment. . . . Am I?

The Rose Diary

May 10, 1979; Washington, D.C.

Thursday Morning. The Tenth Day of the Season.

At 10:00 A.M. San Dominica time, 9:00 A.M.
in Washington, Mrs. Susan Chaplin sat out in the

charming garden cafe of the Gralyn Hotel on N Street.

Mrs. Chaplin wore a cream blouse with matching scarf; a navy skirt; blue-and-white spectators; big sunglasses pushed back on her hair.

She was toying with warm baking-powder biscuits, creamed finnan haddie, and a London prostitute who went by the stage name Betsy Port-Smithe.

Mrs. Susan Chaplin was the stage name for Carrie Rose.

"What I have in mind," Carrie explained, watching a Washington hippie eat an impossibly stuffed Blimpie on the other side of beautifully sculpted hedges, "is a little, uhm, unusual. . . ."

"Unusual?" Port-Smithe shrugged. "Well, let's see. I'm too young, and too good, to get beat up for it. That means *any* sum of money, Mrs. Chaplin . . . what is unusual?" The tall, sandy-haired woman started to laugh. "You want me to pop out of a charlotte russe at someone's fund-raising dinner?"

Carrie Rose began to laugh, too.

When Port-Smithe began to giggle, some of the other patrons of the garden cafe began to sneak glances at the two of them. The young women were framed against a background of plain green umbrellas and the beginnings of Georgetown. Both looked very much a part of the expensive, former embassy scene at the Gralyn. From the look of them, the two women might even be sisters. The resemblance was startling.

An attentive waiter slipped away their breakfast plates (fish, bran flakes, porridge). He placed plump grapes and shiny pears at the center of the table.

"Some time in the next week," Carrie (Mrs. Chaplin) continued when the laughing had stopped, "my husband, Damian, is due to arrive here in Washington. He's coming directly from an obnoxious, hectic, brutal series of business conferences in the Caribbean. . . . Damian sells clothes. Expensive women's clothes.

"At any rate, for some private reasons, I can't be here to meet him. At least I can't *wait* around here for the entire week. . . ."

Port-Smithe sat with a plump grape ready to be popped into her pouty mouth. "And? . . ."

"I'd like you to meet Damian for me. . . . I'd like you to meet him at the St. James, and stay with him a night if I'm not here. That's all."

"Do you know how much I might charge?" Betsy Port-Smithe asked. "For a week of waiting around?"

"I don't. But I'll pay you two hundred a day. Plus your room at the St. James. Plus your food. . . . You're free as a bird until Damian comes. You can even work, if you like. I mean, I realize you're very good, Betsy. That's the whole idea."

The London call girl smiled. She thought that she had it figured out now. . . . This prissy young American wife was looking for some kind of ménage à trois. She just didn't have the nerve to ask for it. . . . Well, fine and dandy.

"To Damian." Port-Smithe raised a cup of coffee with eau-de-vie.

"To Damian." Carrie Rose smiled demurely. She was beginning to get a very good feeling about the way things were breaking on her side of the partnership.

That afternoon she had to fly out of Dulles International.

To Zurich.

To money, power, and those wonderful little munchkins who make the world run so fast and furiously.

Carrie was well aware that she had only one day left now. Approximately thirty hours to outwit several self-acclaimed geniuses, all of them male.

Coastown, San Dominica

They had carefully hidden Peter Macdonald in an expensive suite at the posh Coastown Golf and Racquet Condominiums.

A minimum of five CIA operatives—top men in the Caribbean account—ate, slept, and read *Pent-*

house and Alistair Maclean novels in the seven-room suite with him.

As many as eight agents were there the first day. Three times that many rode pink-canopied golf carts around the manicured lawns all through the night. It was an accepted fact that it would take an army to get Macdonald out of there alive.

Up to his chest in steaming water in the pink marble bathtub, Peter floated quietly in one of the three condominium bathrooms. There was a strange feeling in his head. . . . He'd actually felt his mind go snap Wednesday afternoon.

Standing beside the *Fish 'n Fool*, the black policeman holding him by both shoulders, whispering loudly, "Jane was killed this morning. I'm very sorry, mister."

Snap.

Like breaking a bone, tearing a tendon. Never knowing before that his head was so fragile.

It wasn't exactly that he wouldn't be able to exist without Janie. He would. Had for twenty-odd years before he met her. . . . It was more that he didn't think he could be completely sane without her. . . .

Sane was something he'd never been particularly good at, anyway. Sane. Coping; content; not painfully lonely; not jumping into West Point because you think it will make your father love you.

Six-fifteen A.M. on his old Timex. Ten days since it all began.

Red sun shooting streaks through a louvered bathroom window. Somebody already playing tennis outside . . . *bonk* . . . *bonk* . . . *bonk* . . . undoubtedly more agents. . . .

They'd tried awfully hard to be nice. The San Dominican police. CIA. They'd left him pretty much by himself the night before. Not bugged him with too many questions. . . .

He'd sat alone in a dark bedroom in the condominium most of the night. Big New York–cut steak untouched on a tray. Asparagus tips. Strawberry parfait sundae. Feeling like a little kid left alone in a big house. Having some kind of bizarre Kodachrome-quality memory of the first time he and Janie had been together. A three-day cross-island trip while they were still practically strangers. The kind of great, dopey, romantic stuff that could happen only in a vacation spot. Making him cry, he missed her so badly.

Peter turned his body in the hot, soapy tub. The hot water felt unreal in the rush of air-conditioning. Like lying under the covers with the window open in winter . . . everything weird, and unreal, and impossible to relate to.

His mind had just gone snap. Snap, crackle, pop. Peter didn't give a shit. He did: but he didn't.

What he wanted now—what he'd been thinking about since late last night—was how he could get his revenge. Everything was beautifully simple, for a change. Just one guiding light. Get the blond mercenary somehow. Blow his brains out. Just like Jane, only slower.

Sitting in the bathtub, Peter figured out one other important thing. He figured that he probably wouldn't have to worry about looking for the blond Englishman. One day he'd look up—and the blond man would just be there. Just like at Turtle Bay.

At nine o'clock Damian sat inside a Coastown church and carefully studied the place.

A small black boy came up to him, and Damian made the most horrifying face he could imagine. The boy laughed like a banshee. Visitors in the church turned to complain, then they began to smile, too.

Meanwhile the hired English killer was accelerating the merry wild-mouse chase around San Dominica.

He was also managing to round out Damian's flat and, until then, rather bloodless character. Clive Lawson was getting Rose labeled as a first-class pervert.

Sitting on one of the stonework terraces of the ramshackle Royal Caribbean Hotel, Lawson eyed a cocky little stinkpot chugging up toward Coastown under big mackerel clouds.

In a dilapidated white-wicker chair two feet across from him, a naked, mewing seventeen-year-old was expounding some sort of psychedelic swami—Moon—Castaneda gibberish about organic orgasms. The adult-breasted teen had gray streaks in very long black hair. Her face was long, too, spare and striking.

"Like . . . like saffron and ocher paints . . . are like mixing on the insides of my eyelids," she said in a whispery voice that made the revelation sexy if nothing else.

Meanwhile she stuck two long fingers deep inside herself.

Clive Lawson watched the girl's fingers work back and forth, back and forth, like two long legs walking in dune grass. Very slowly he masturbated himself with both hands.

The girl's name was Stormy Lascher. Half of her brain had been blasted away by acid and psilocybin; the other half departed while she was working at a massage parlor inside New York's once mediocre Commodore Hotel.

The blond Englishman, she was discovering—chauvinist and dirty old thirty-three-year-old that he was—also had an interesting (blue-veined, cockyhatted, well-muscled) Capricorn prick. In fact, his standard equipment compared favorably with the slimmer, cuter rocketships on so many of the college boys from nearby Sunshower Beach.

"I'm going to come any sec," the seventeen-year-old screamed, pointing her dirty silver-toed feet up like a ballet dancer. "Oh, Jesus. Jesus Christ."

Stormy started to shiver, moan, and she brought a long tab of amyl nitrite up to her little pug nose. As she broke open the tab, she heard the blond man say very clearly, "I'm the one they're looking for. The Englishman. Now there's one for your record book, Storm."

The long-haired girl nodded her head once—then nothing but bright, mixing paints were there.

By ten A.M. the English killer was on the road up to Coastown, heading toward another of his targets.

By ten Denise "Stormy" Lascher was sitting out on the terrace of room 334, screaming like the hopeless madwoman she would one day become.

At a little after eleven the police, the army, and the CIA swarmed over the Royal Caribbean like ants on a gingerbread castle. Harold Hill and Brooks Campbell marched through the ornate front lobby together, Campbell carrying a bulky M-16 rifle. The police stopped all regular elevator service and began to search the ancient, sprawling dinosaur from the cellar up to the gabled rooftops.

Hill, Campbell, and Dr. Johnson went directly to room 334, where Denise Lascher was being detained. The hysterical teenager told them that the man must have left before all the police came bursting in. She didn't know for sure. . . . Yes, he was tall. Blond-haired. Like Michael Caine, she said.

No, she didn't remember anything specific he'd said. Just that he was the one . . . the machete killer everyone was looking for.

Harold Hill rummaged through the trash baskets in the suite's bedroom and bath. The gray-haired CIA director found empty, crushed packs of Dunhill cigarettes, marijuana roaches, an empty carton for Remington rifle shells, a box of French ticklers. Garbage.

Meanwhile Meral Johnson had put out an alert for the car the tall blond man had been seen driving. A blue 1979 Mustang, license number 3984-A, according to the hotel register.

Johnson sent his men and the American inspectors around the hotel to interview as many of the guests and help as possible. At the same time he had roadblocks set up outside Carolinsted and all through the surrounding villages.

Dr. Johnson had the feeling that they might finally be closing in on him. The black man hadn't slept for two days now; he was obsessed with getting the blond mercenary. More so than any of them, he believed privately . . . Johnson alone understood that the tall blond man had destroyed San Dominica.

In front of the hotel, Campbell and Harold Hill leaned on a driftwood fence railing, both of them chain-smoking.

"I haven't known what to say about Carole."

Campbell flipped his cigarette onto the beach sand. "I'm sorry. I hope you know how I feel, Harry."

"You feel that you have to say something," Harold Hill said, and smiled cruelly. "That's all you feel, Brooks."

Campbell let his eyes drift out over the soothing, beautiful Caribbean. "What about Macdonald?"

"If we catch Rose, Macdonald makes the ID. I'd hate to do it off that photokit drawing. . . . I'm also prepared to try him as bait for Rose. If we can be clever enough to do that discreetly."

"I think Rose might try to hit Macdonald anyway. What else is keeping him around here?"

Harold Hill extended his hands, palms up. He didn't know.

The two men walked back across the hotel's rolling lawns. As they approached a waiting Puma helicopter, men in blue jumpsuits began to take off the plane's chocks and hawsers.

"We're getting very close to him now," Harold Hill said, "or vice versa."

At eleven o'clock Peter made the first of four tape recordings for the CIA's more than 8.5-billion-item computer files.

For an hour and a half straight he talked into a reel-to-reel Sony for the edification of two very hip academic-type interrogators from Washington. He told them about his odyssey through the West Hills jungle; about everything he'd seen at Turtle Bay; about his feelings toward the U.S. government after Watergate; after Cambodia; after, say, Jane had been killed. . . .

In short, the two interrogators were trying to determine whether Peter was going to give them any trouble.

At twelve-thirty a police artist started a photokit drawing of Damian Rose, based on what Peter could remember from the unbelievable fifteen-second tableau on the Shore Highway.

By one o'clock his interrogators were in the offices of Alcoa Aluminum, color copying a fair likeness of the tall blond man.

Also at one o'clock, Peter asked the CIA for a gun to protect himself, but he was refused.

At two a crowd of agents removed him from the Golf and Racquet Condominiums. Things were going too fast all of a sudden. Everything fuzzy and unclear.

They took an elevator two floors down to the lobby. Then a fast walk through a garden—to a gray Ford with little American flags on the fenders. Switched back two cars to a blue Mercury Cougar with the shiniest front grille in captivity.

Doors shut like clockwork, then the blue Mercury jerked away from the curb. Flashed past palm trees and stately casuarinas. Tires screeched out onto Orange Boulevard, where unconcerned blacks sold bananas and papaya on the sidewalks.

Off to the Church of Angels. Off to see a lot of the victims, including Jane.

Sitting in back—arms folded, mind folded—Peter wondered why they had decided to go to the church in broad daylight. He forgot the thought momentarily. Saw Jane blinking on and off like neon lights. Saw the blond man over Turtle Bay. Saw himself on the flashy green Peugeot bicycle.

"You all right, Pete?"

"Yeah. Sure. I was just thinking. . . ."

Inside the medium-size Catholic church, Harold Hill and Brooks Campbell waited in the sacristy. Both Washington men were wearing lightweight business suits; they looked appropriately respectful.

They were discussing important logistics with an oblate priest, Father Kevin Brennan. They wanted to know where all the side and back doors were. Where the press could get their photographs but not get in the way. Where an assassin—"if an assassin had it in mind, Father"—might try to hide inside the church.

Meanwhile a crowd from the streets was starting to gather and move inside the front doors of the church. The crowd also included both Clive Lawson and Damian Rose.

As the government car swept around the church's circular driveway, Peter couldn't help thinking that

the baby cathedral wasn't a bad place for a sniper.
Ugly deranged crowd; busy city streets; lots of carnival confusion.

Stepping out of the official-looking Mercury, he
heard the crowd's loud chant.

"United. State. Murderers!

"United. State. Murderers!

"Haile Selassie!

"Haile Selassie!"

He watched a blur of black faces craning long
necks, bulging veins, trying to find out what was
going on all over their island.

It was so goddamn weird. A lot like Saigon in
'73. It made Peter feel like getting up with a microphone—explaining that most people in the United
States were okay. That they didn't want all the island's bauxite—they didn't want to hurt anybody.
Period.

Five men in dark suits and crisp white shirts met
him on the creaking front steps of the church.
Brooks Campbell. Dr. Johnson. Harold Hill. The
American ambassador himself.

A young Catholic priest took Peter by the arm.
Brief condolences and clumsy apologies were ex-
changed. Then the entourage quickly moved inside.

A TV news cameraman followed close behind
them, stumbling along like a proud uncle at a wedding.

Two marines followed with MAT submachine guns.

Meanwhile Peter had put on his old baseball hat. Like Green Berets wearing their hats to funerals. Fuck your silly rules; conventions; fuck you!

"Not in here, Peter," the priest whispered. "The hat. Please."

Peter heard nothing but the sound of two rows of plain wooden coffins being lined up in front of the church's central altar. The boxes contained bodies still unclaimed after the Elizabeth's Fancy massacre. They held the two dead agents from Mandeville Hospital. One of the temporary Red Cross coffins held Jane.

"I know how you feel, Peter. But you're showing disrespect for Our Lord in this way."

"I doubt it means diddly-shit one way or the other to Our Lord. If it does, I don't buy his act, either."

Finally Father Brennan pointed to a particular coffin to the right of the bright gold-and-red altar.

Peter stopped in front of a coffin with a place card: JANE FRANCES COOKE.

He looked down the line of U.S. embassy and police officials. Praying? Reciting the Pledge of Allegiance? . . . The scene reminded him of the aftermath of some large tragedy he'd seen in some news clip. Hundreds of bodies laid out in a grammar school cafeteria. Mourners searching for friends and relatives. Violated in their grief by television cameras.

"Aren't you going to open it?" he finally said to the priest. "I'd like to see her once more, please."

"We haven't been doing that," the priest said in a whisper. "These aren't the best conditions, Peter."

"I'd like to see her. I think we can all take it."

"Will you take off your hat?" the priest asked again.

Peter took off the baseball hat, and the oblate consented to lift the lid for a brief viewing. It wasn't what he thought best—but the police chief said yes; the American ambassador said yes; and the young American man seemed to know what he wanted. . . .

With a loud tearing noise, the lid came off.

Peter looked down and saw a young-looking woman, only vaguely recognizable, surprisingly small now. . . . Jane had been prepared with what looked like an old lady's face powder and rouge. Her long blond curls looked brittle and stiff, like the artificial hair on a child's doll. They hadn't even used one of her own dresses. . . .

Oh, my God, no, Peter said over and over to himself. *Oh, God, Jesus. Goddammit. Goddammit.* If all those bastards hadn't been watching him, he would have let himself cry.

At the same time, Damian was watching the English killer, high up in the church's choir loft. He was just three aisles behind Clive Lawson. No more than twelve feet away.

The expensive killer had had one opportunity, but he'd resisted it. Basically a good decision, Rose was thinking, calculating. This church was an interesting place for a shot, spectacular and unexpected—a thrill kill—but maybe it wasn't the best place. Nonetheless, I would have done it here, Damian thought. Maybe on the way out. . . .

He studied Peter Macdonald standing in front of his girlfriend's coffin; he watched Brooks Campbell, Hill—ducks on a pond.

Soon, however, he saw Clive Lawson quietly leave the choir loft, then the church altogether. The English killer had on a dark, contemporary rug that made him look like many of the news reporters. Like the Secret Service men, for that matter. Not bad for a traveling disguise.

It appeared that the grand finale, the coup de grace, was going to have to wait just a little bit longer.

Damian left the Church of Angels with the main body of the crowd. He was an odd-looking sight with his baggy yellow trousers; his parasol; his jester's cap held respectfully in one hand.

Almost instantly he was accosted by a mob of kids who wanted to play with Basil, the Children's Minstrel.

Thursday Evening.

All Thursday, San Dominica had been overturned and researched as desperately as it should have been the very night of the Elizabeth's Fancy massacre.

Owners of stores, cafes, taverns, and private homes were badgered by agents with the photokit drawing made from Peter's description.

Each and every motel, hotel, inn, chalet, hacienda, villa, lodge, casa, caravansary—black or white in clientele—all were assaulted by marauding teams of local police and U.S. federal marshals. Rude Boys were hired to go out and mine for information in the larger city underworlds; among the cocaine and ganja dealers. Thousands of ordinary people were held up at the airports and boat docks, as well as at the major roadblocks set all over the island.

Neither Damian Rose nor Clive Lawson turned up in any of the searches, however. Like a Martin Bormann, a Mengele—they were simply not the type of fish that wind up in a police dragnet.

Bay of Pigs II was fast becoming Bay of Panic.

At 7:00 P.M. that night, a communications expert, Harvey Epstein, thought that he'd lucked into the first gold strike of the entire manhunt.

At the time of the discovery, Epstein was playing

Canfield solitaire on the floor of a VW van. The van was parked about three hundred yards behind a large villa owned by the Charles Forlenza Family (Sunasta Hotels) on San Dominica. Inside the van, Epstein was illegally bugging the Forlenza phones.

For two straight days now the only thing he'd heard was the Forlenza cook calling in her giggly orders for groceries at a place called the Coastown Gourmet Market. When the phone rang at seven, Harvey had a hunger attack.

He pressed his earphones to one ear only, uncovered a club ace. Listened.

"Hello."

The first voice he recorded was a hood named Duane Nicholson. Nicholson was the man Isadore Goldman had brought with him to Government House on May 6.

Epstein assumed that the second voice was that of Damian Rose.

"I'm going to need those favors done for me," Rose said. "Put your part of things into operation."

"Tomorrow, right?" Nicholson asked.

Click. Buzz.

"Son of a bitch. Harvey! Son of a bitch!"

In less than an hour Campbell and Harold Hill were listening to the tape in Coastown.

"Interesting." Campbell recognized the silky voice. "It was Rose."

Still under guard at the Golf and Racquet Club,

Peter sat in front of the San Dominican Broadcasting Corporation's blurry evening news.

For the first time in two days he was clear-headed enough to consider the effect of a sniper's bullet. Every president's daydream . . . your car windshield splattered against a bug. Half an ounce of steel entering your forehead at three thousand feet per second. Insane and nauseating.

Around 8:30 he made a phone call to his family in Grand Rapids.

His mother couldn't understand why air force one hadn't flown him home already. "Make them put you on the first plane out of that place," Betsy Macdonald told Peter. "My God, they've put you through enough already. They can come right up here to ask you any more questions they have. Tell them that, Peter. . . ."

Peter's father wanted to know what the real story was. He'd talked to his friend Senator Pflanzer, and Pflanzer wanted to know, too. "Pete, don't take any chances for those sorry bastards," Colonel Edward Macdonald said—Big Mac. "They're not doing shit for us anymore—the whole damn government. They don't deserve anything back from us. I mean it."

As he listened, occasionally talked, Peter tried to picture Big Mac and Little Betsy. He saw them maybe ten years younger than they really were now.

He saw the Super Six posing like some roughneck hockey team.

"I'll try to get home real soon," he said to his father. "Tell that to Mom. Tell my brothers, too. Miss the hell out of all of you. I really do."

After the call, Peter just sat in the dark pseudotropics condominium bedroom. Thinking.

He imagined a slow-motion pistol shot to a man's forehead. Like the famous Vietnamese execution photograph. The tall blond man's head actually vaporizing.

At 1:30 in the morning one of the CIA agents came into the bedroom—a little Italian guy who was always imitating Peter Falk.

"We're going to move you, Pete. Get ready, will you?"

Getting dressed, Peter prepared himself mentally. No point in getting scared now. Scared or stupid . . . maybe there was, but fuck it.

Three agents with automatic rifles walked him to a station wagon waiting outside with the motor running.

A quick breath of fresh air. Appropriately fishy smell of the sea. No *ca-rack* of a rifle from the dark palm trees.

They rode to the Dorcas Hotel in Coastown in eerie silence. No questions asked; no information volunteered. No phony-baloney bullshit on their side or his.

The gray-haired CIA man—Harold Hill—was waiting for him inside the new hotel suite. A pleasant enough place—like a Holiday Inn.

"My family has put in a formal complaint to the State Department." Peter lied simply and effectively. "It went through Senator Pflanzer," he announced to Hill and to Brooks Campbell, who were sitting in the living room. "If you don't give me a crack at the blond mystery man, I'm going to force you to send me home. You know the tune—'War Hero Claims CIA Monkeyshines!' "

"All right, all right." The gray-haired man nodded. A very sober professor type, Peter noticed. "Let's sit down and talk, Peter."

By 2:00 A.M. Peter Macdonald was officially part of the manhunt for Damian and Carrie Rose.

Shortly afterward the fat black police chief arrived at the Dorcas. Strange man! Dr. Johnson just sat around talking with Peter. About the initial mistake by his constable at Turtle Bay; his own mistakes during the difficult case; the night he'd spent with Jane at Mandeville Hospital.

"I couldn't sleep at home," the likable San Dominican finally said. "I thought you might understand."

"I understand." Peter smiled. "I think this is going to be an awfully long night. Glad you're here, Dr. Johnson."

CHAPTER TWENTY-SEVEN

Damian had gotten uncharacteristically
grubby—vacant-eyed and distracted
during the last months of our preparation
for San Dominica. His hair was hardly ever
combed. He spent entire days inside the
house, wandering in wrinkled silk
pajamas. He was obsessed with the idea
of master criminals. . . . I came home one
night to find him reading a book called <u>On
Aggression</u>, babbling about brown rats
and piebald eagles. Another time he was
reading <u>The Rise and Fall of the Third
Reich</u>. Lots of Nazi books after that. The
Master Criminal Race, he called them. . . .

The Rose Diary

Trelawney, San Dominica

In a small den lit by a black-and-white TV, Damian sat cleaning an M-21 sniper's rifle.

First he pressed out the rear pin and opened the rifle. Then he withdrew the bolt and bolt carrier assembly. He withdrew the thin firing retaining pin. Withdrew the cam pin, the bolt from the bolt carrier.

On and off he watched Alfred Hitchcock's *Notorious* coming over the island's erratic TV network. Overall, Damian decided, he could have been a much better performer than the very one-dimensional Cary Grant. He wasn't certain if he could have been as good as a Claude Rains or an Ingrid Bergman, though. Those two were perfectionists. They could have made something out of Basil, the Children's Minstrel.

When the rifle was cleaned, when the M-21 was all back together, he went into the bathroom, where he worked for another hour or so. Using a mixture of Quiet Touch and Miss Clairol, he dyed his hair what the package called "blue black," with gray highlights. Damian's own hair color.

Now there was only one tall blond Englishman: Clive Lawson.

And only one more day.

Before Damian Rose called it a night, he took a new field machete out of its cheesecloth wrapping. He laid the knife out carefully by his rifle.

Then the tall black-haired American went off to sleep.

PART III

The Perfect Ending

May 11, 1979, Friday
Shoot-Out!
4
Die

May 11, 1979; Coastown, San Dominica

Friday Morning. The Last Day of the Season.

Dr. Johnson broke open a croissant, dabbed half of the crisp roll with guava jelly, watched Peter out of the corner of his eye.

"What a damn wonderful time for living it could have been." Peter shook his head as he spoke to the fat black policeman.

The young American man was looking *especially* American in the bright light of morning. He was wearing a forest green (holey, punky) SEE BEAR MOUNTAIN T-shirt; wrinkled athletic shorts; no shoes or socks; his ratty old baseball hat.

He was rubbing his bare feet together like sticks trying to make a fire.

"Swimming." He continued on with his spiel. "Sailing. Playing basketball, if you're a recidivist like me . . . running around in a baseball cap like you're ten years old again and don't care . . . all kinds of wonderful, life-wasting crap. Nothing too serious, you know, R and R.''

The middle-aged police chief was beginning to feel very tired, depressed. He kept remembering the night he spent in the hospital with the blond girl. Moreover he was beginning to feel paternal toward the young American. He liked Peter. Sometimes he felt it was them against all the rest.

"This island used to be that way. When I was a boy. I don't know if the world will let you do that anymore. Be carefree."

Peter nodded without saying anything.

He and the police chief were sitting under a striped yellow umbrella on a sixteenth-floor terrace of the Dorcas Hotel. Across the terrace from them, two CIA men stood by the railing with their suit jackets off, old-fashioned shoulder holsters strapped across their white shirts. Behind them, Coastown stretched out like a giant, glittering carnival. One story above, the roof of the Dorcas was yellow, the color of gold teeth. The sloping roof was too steep for anyone to climb on, someone who knew about such things had decided.

Peter threw back his head and looked around and around a cloudless, china blue skyscape. He started to think about heroes, leaders, inspiration. . . . Once, when he was a plebe, he remembered going to a humanities symposium: "Is the Hero Dead in Western Civilization?" Four history and classics professors answered—shouted to the rafters—"Yes! Yes! Dead and buried!"

Well, dammit, people still needed heroes. He did, anyway . . . Ulysses, Churchill, Lincoln . . . whoever! Somebody! That unbelievable ass Nixon. Gerry Ford. Jesus! Didn't they know anything about being leaders? Heroes? . . . If Kissinger could get to be a sex object, Richard Nixon could have at least gotten up to the level of human being.

"Man, oh, man, oh, man," he said in rhythm with his neck and head circles. "It's so damn unbelievable, isn't it? Worse than Vietnam, and that really sucked. Bad, Meral, bad. . . . I keep fantasizing that Janie is going to be alive again."

Trelawney, San Dominica

Damian Rose passed the first three hours of the morning struggling to fix a badly misused twenty-five-foot Bertram Sportsman.

Naked to the waist, dressed only in striped cotton pants, he worked on the speedboat's trimplanes first; then replaced all the plugs; then did what he could about the engine's timing.

The Caribbean was a pretty dark blue in the early morning. The cove where he worked was A Technicolor blur. Fuzzy blue-and-gold-and-white brilliance. Like movies shot through a Vaseline-covered lens.

The cove was also neatly hidden from passing sea traffic; a little dogleg right behind a hill thick with palmettos.

Tucked up in the hills behind the cove was the home of a famous Caribbean landscape painter, the old recluse Eric Downes. Hidden in a closet with stacks of bare canvases, Downes now lay dead.

As he tuned the boat's engine, Damian's mind slipped back and forth between the Caribbean and France. Between the start of this working year and the end of it. . . . He remembered walks with Carrie through the Luxembourg Gardens; whole afternoons wasted in the Tuileries, the Place des Vosges, cafe sitting around St.-Germain-des-Prés.

After he finished the engine work, Rose took an extra gas tank and two M-21 rifles down below into the cabin. He left the new field machete up in the cockpit.

When he finally looked at his watch, he was surprised to see that it was nearly nine. That meant Carrie ought to be on her way to Morocco.

As he settled down to wait, Damian began to whistle sweet "Lili Marlene." A truly great song. A tune that never failed to remind him of Carrie.

Zurich, Switzerland

Wearing a blue-gray shift and gray Valentino turban, she sat across from a red-mustached, very fat munchkin, S. O. Rogin, in the Schweizer Kreditverein in Zurich.

A soft leather Hermès attaché case lay on a heavy marble table between them. Over their heads a crystal chandelier provided adequate light, though filled with a blizzard of dust motes.

Rogin spoke English with a thick German-Swiss accent with one bushy eyebrow curiously arched. "You wish to withdraw all six hundred twenty-nine thousand?"

Carrie considered the question for a moment. "Yes. All of it," she then said. Very businesslike.

"Very well, then. All right. How would you like your money?"

The American woman took out a blue pack of cigarettes—Gauloises. The banker produced a klunky silver lighter. As Rogin lit her cigarette, a strong smell of kerosene wafted up. Then the lighter clicked shut like an aspirin tin.

"What would you suggest?" Carrie asked.

The fat munchkin began to grin. "What would I suggest? For starters, I would suggest we transfer the funds directly to your new bank. *Tout de suite*, Mrs. Chaplin. Easy as apple pie. No suitcases."

"No. I'm afraid I must have the cash in hand, Herr Rogin."

"Hmmm. Of course." The redheaded man nodded. "Will madame be needing a security guard, then? I will explain to you the simple procedure for—"

"I'll be fine." Carrie smiled, effectively cutting off the man. "If you read in *New Zurchen* about someone murdered in the streets downtown," she went on, "you'll know that someone tried to take away my money."

The munchkin—an American and British detective fan—laughed with genuine good humor. "No one is ever murdered in Zurich, madame. Not in that manner, anyway." The banker laughed once again. Then he left to arrange for the six hundred twenty-nine thousand—one million five hundred thousand in Swiss francs.

As he walked through the elegant bank, S. O. Rogin wondered if the pretty lady was running away from her husband. He viewed Mrs. Chaplin as a sort of . . . Faye Dunaway type. The fat man recalled Miss Dunaway in a scene from *Windmills of the Mind*. No, no. From *The Thomas Crown Affair*. A wonderful escapist movie. All about robbing the banks of Boston.

Forty minutes later Carrie Rose walked out of the Kreditverein with the Hermès briefcase full of Swiss francs. She was beginning to perspire now;

her skin was prickling. She was paranoid about strangers on the Zurich streets.

The tall, long-haired American woman went just one block across the Stampfenbachstrasse, however. She entered the impressive Union Bank of Switzerland and redeposited the cash.

All part of the master plan.

Chapter Twenty-eight

> Sooner or later, we were certain they
> would throw Macdonald to us. Harold Hill
> was an executive: good executives are
> executors. Predictable because they try to
> be so logical. . . . Damian never tries to
> figure out the mazes, just the mice. . . .
>
> The Rose Diary

Wahoo Cay, San Dominica

Friday Afternoon.

At two in the hot, hot of the afternoon, Damian
floated over an exquisite range of shallow barrier
reefs.

Sunbathing in the twenty-five-foot Sportsman,
watching mullets and snipe eels forage and dart
through the bottle green waters, he was beginning
to let his mind drift to thoughts of meeting Carrie.

Seedy Morocco. Casbahs. A perfect ending for this crime. The two who got away with it.

Damian was convinced that San Dominica represented the best freelance work done since John Kennedy was hit in Dallas. He knew it.

Just a few more hours to go now. All of it heading helter-skelter yet inevitably toward a small pinprick in time and space.

Actually, the end began in a most understated manner, a curious contrast to everything that had gone before it.

At 3:15 Dr. Meral Johnson and Brooks Campbell escorted Peter out of the Dorcas Hotel.

The young American man was wearing gray cotton pants with a loose-fitting gray zipper jacket. Underneath the jacket was a German semiautomatic pistol. The Walther was a neat, tough gun. Compliments of Great Western Air Transport, of Harold Hill in particular.

The three men got into a wide Dodge Charger idling in the hotel carport. Campbell looked around for rooftop snipers, and that seemed almost funny to Peter. "Uh, that's *our* fort," he finally had to say.

From the hotel they drove to a secluded villa owned by the Charles Forlenza Family. A big flamingo pink Hollywood-style house.

Both Campbell and Harold Hill had hopes now that the man staying at the villa—Duane Nicholson—would either contact, or be contacted by, Damian Rose. They'd put a five-car stakeout team on the house.

Officially, Peter was along to make any necessary identification. Officially, he didn't have a gun.

Unofficially, Harold Hill was beginning to troll bait for Rose.

In some ways he too was reminded of the November of 1963. Very messy stuff. A marvel how you could smooth out these things in the end—national security matters.

At six o'clock in Washington, a Mrs. C. Rose checked into the St. James Hotel. Some mail was waiting for her—letters from Damian. Very mushy and adolescent, Port-Smithe thought.

At seven o'clock in Zurich, Carrie waited in her hotel suite. She watched swans glide over the lake of Zurich, made casual notes for the diary, tried to take care of all the final details the way Damian would. . . .

At a quarter to eight, a chip of burnt-orange sun sank without a trace behind the Forlenza villa.

His heart started to thump out strange warnings as Peter watched Isadore Goldman's expensive lackey walk outside the big stucco house. He considered that Isadore Goldman was just a name to him; considered that he really didn't want to die. He wanted to shoot the tall blond mercenary somehow; wanted to go home to Michigan again. Like thriller-chiller novel endings.

"Blue. This is White Flag," Brooks Campbell whispered into the car's crackling shortwave radio. "You guys all awake?"

"Peter?" Meral Johnson winked into the car's rearview mirror. "Awake?"

"He's just going out for a roast beef on rye," Peter said, feeling electricity, anyway. "I'm wide-awake, Meral." He grinned at the fat policeman. Neither of them talked to Campbell.

Easygoing and, to Peter's eyes, unconcerned, Duane Nicholson shuffled across the villa's front lawn in Indian moccasins, casual slacks, some sort of sky blue surfer's shirt. A very expendable type, Peter couldn't help thinking. The kind of guy who always got shot first in adventure movies. Having walked the length of the house, the curly-headed hood disappeared into a dark three-car garage.

Minutes later a dull-white Corvette rolled out onto the driveway. Low slung on the driver's seat, resting comfortably behind a stained pigskin steering wheel, the Las Vegas mobster wheeled the powerful car out to the dirt access road. Then bolting and roaring like an animal that wasn't used to restraints, the Corvette chugged toward the Shore Highway.

Izzie Goldman's man was heading into Coast-own.

Sitting on the backseat of one of five surveillance cars, Peter had already clicked his mind into combat readiness. Just in case. He figured the punk hoodlum was going to dinner, though. Everyone in the surveillance cars figured the same thing.

Tryall, San Dominica

A shadowy figure thrusted itself up a long sliver of dock due west of Coastown's twinkling pocket of electric lights.

To the running man's back, dark tuna boats lay on the horizon of the Caribbean. Beyond the fishing boats were several thousand miles of open sea. Then the southern extremes of Europe.

For this last night on San Dominica, Damian Rose had chosen a beige security guard's uniform. Pitch black makeup was smeared on his face and hands so that from a distance he looked like a native. An M-21 with a complicated-looking sight was slung over his left shoulder; a heavy sugar-cane machete was tied to his waist.

Looking both ways and back over his shoulder first, he started across a wide field toward a distant, narrow road.

Peter glanced at his watch: 8:35.

The Chevrolet Corvette and three surveillance cars were creeping slowly down Charles Henry

Street on the northern outskirts of Coastown. The cars slunk up a crowded side avenue with old wrecks of American autos lined along both sides. Black children in colorful rags darted in and out of the parked cars. Slouch-hatted Rude Boys whacked the hoods of the passing night traffic.

The dusty Corvette swept up a dark, crowded lane that looped around and then ran alongside Queen Anne's Park. The park was still jam-packed with laughing, running blacks practicing for Labor Day Carnival, the official end of the tourist season.

"He's on to us," Brooks Campbell whispered inside the white Charger. "What the fuck is that bastard doing?"

On the side of a damp, grassy hill, Damian Rose waited calmly with his M-21 and machete. Not sixty yards away, completely unaware of Rose, Clive Lawson stood with an Uzi submachine gun resting on his hip. He too waited.

On the backseat of the Charger, Peter was absorbing flashing pieces of Queen Anne's Park. Nearly subliminal stuff. Men and boys in flowing white shirts. Dancing bonfires. A few purplish clouds moving fast in a high wind. . . . It was a little like being on patrol—a strange, worthless night patrol dreamed up by the usual morons. Shoot anyone who doesn't answer to the name *Carl Yastrzemski*.

"He's leading us to the tall blond man." Peter

answered Campbell's earlier question. "He's doing exactly what you wanted him to do. . . . All we have to do is figure out why."

Just then the Corvette swung wide around a big City of Coastown truck. The Corvette took an impossibly sharp, skidding left—then the low-slung car started to accelerate up a hill as if it were flat ground.

"Brace yourselves, gentlemen," Meral Johnson yelled out.

The steep hill came and went—then swept down roller-coaster style on quiet, narrow side streets.

An unofficial Grand Prix race was beginning. People along the sidewalks were screaming at the fast-moving, souped-up cars.

Eight thirty-nine. Damian checked the M-21 carefully. Checked the ammo.

Clive Lawson still had the submachine gun on his hip.

His stomach floating up in his chest cavity, his heart pounding like a tight bass drum, Peter watched Isadore Goldman's man shoot down a narrow, unmarked driveway.

"White Flag" nearly missed it.

A green Mazda missed; spun off into berry bushes. Harold Hill's blue Cougar made the hairpin turn in the middle of the road.

Another quick right turn followed in unfair progression. An immediate impossible left. Then a frightening straight, four-block-long speedway appeared out of nowhere.

One catch: the speedway was blanketed with people.

From the bouncing rear seat, Peter watched a blur of panic-stricken blacks running wildly. They'd been loitering around the street, catching the cool breeze. . . . Now they were diving onto the dirt sidewalks. A few crazy ones seemed to be imitating toreadors, flapping shirts and sweaters at the passing, weaving cars. A woman was hit—*bang*.

Eight forty-three.

Inside the white Charger, Brooks Campbell unholstered his revolver. Dr. Johnson was sitting on the car horn—creating one sustained scream.

The Corvette twitched into third. Then up into fourth gear.

Peter took his gun out of his shoulder holster. Semiautomatic Walther. Tough gun.

The low-slung sports car opened up nearly a two-block lead on the others. It was getting small fast. A white box and flashing taillights—hugging the road—leaving the city like a ground rocket.

Then Brooks Campbell was screaming, pointing at the Corvette, which was suddenly way over on the right.

The Corvette was jetting down a dark country road. Opening up a quarter-mile lead.

Clive Lawson was getting the Uzi ready now. He

planted his feet in the soft dirt of the hillside. He stretched his arms, right first, then left.

"We're losing him, goddammit. We're losing him!"

The fat, sweating police chief twirled the steering wheel. The white Charger spun. Turned. Just missed turning over. Peter was thrown across the backseat. Felt his head crack against a side window.

They were accelerating down the dark back road with the Corvette completely out of sight now. Brooks Campbell radioing for reinforcements, armies. Asking where the Tryall Road came out. . . .

Eight forty-four. Damian braced the M-21 against a coconut palm. Watched through his nightscope.

Then all of the surveillance cars braked suddenly for a fork around a huge, spreading kapok tree.

"Left! Hill will go—"

The last part of Brooks Campbell's instruction was drowned out. Peter was screaming at Meral Johnson to step on the gas.

Unbelievably, the Dodge Charger's side front window disintegrated.

A high-powered rifle was exploding over and over in the dark woods. Methodical sniping. A professional marksman.

The Charger's roof ripped apart. Another window blew up. The car's trunk took a blast that would have killed an elephant.

Meral Johnson was screaming for Macdonald to stay down.

Somebody's head slammed against a window and broke right through it.

"On the floor! On the floor!"

The roof was hit again. Another blast hit somewhere in the greenhouse—the window frame area. Gun blasts pounded the car like sledgehammers.

At least twenty explosions came within thirty seconds.

Then all was quiet on the dark back road. A magic silence. Millions of twitting bugs. Tropical birds. The transition back and forth was almost incomprehensible.

The wounded Charger was still rolling. Its tires were making pathetic little clicking noises.

Meral Johnson had his hand down on the floor in the front seat. Flat down on the gritty brake pedal. Finally he stopped the Charger.

Men from "Green Flag" were running to help. Bouncing sunglasses. Wingtips slapping on macadam.

Harold Hill was running from way down the road. Screaming something. Looking like the father of a drowning child.

"Macdonald!" the black policeman also suddenly screamed. "Macdonald!"

A low groan came from inside the car.

Peter sat up on the backseat. Started to shake off

glass. Gash in his head, he realized. Blood . . . shit. . . .

He saw Campbell up in front. Looking at the shattered windshield as if he'd finally solved the whole goddamn awful thing.

Except that the Great Western Air Transport man was too dead to solve things anymore.

A revolutionary American-made bullet had pierced one side of the handsome face, tumbled over once, tried to tumble over again—exploded brain matter all over the walls and roof of the man's skull. Like a bulldozer gouging out a small living room.

And then Peter wasn't looking at Campbell anymore. He was running. For the first time since April 25—Turtle Bay—he was moving like a certifiable madman, holding the Walther semiautomatic like a baton in a relay race.

He'd seen the tall blond man up in the woods.

Damian scrutinized Harold Hill and the black police chief in the steaming headlights of the unmarked police cars.

Then Rose retreated farther back into the thick brush and brambles. Back closer to the boat. Escape. Carrie.

Just one more scenario now.

As he pushed his way through dark tree shapes and hanging moss, Peter heard shrieking birds and bugs all around him. The moon seemed to be racing through the shiny leaf ceiling over his head.

After about seventy yards of the restrictive bushes, he emerged into the wide-open space of the Tryall Club's golf course. He could see the Caribbean then, faint line of foamy surf. He could make out the main clubhouse, a long low building with half a hundred windows facing the golf course—closed for the summer season.

Peter's wide eyes methodically searched the dark Tryall golf course. He was in a combat trance now, all his movements automatic: search and destroy, kill the mercenary or get killed.

His eyes ran over the neat, handsome clubhouse; along the dark flagstone patio and walkway; past hedges, gardens; down a long porch filled with rocking chairs.

Somewhere between the bramble and the clubhouse he'd missed a turn by the tall running man. His powers as a tracker of men were rusty, Peter realized—gone altogether, kaput. A good Vietnamese soldier would have killed him by now.

A stitch of white lightning lit up the night sky.

Then Peter heard Meral Johnson's first scream.

Usually more athletic, he took a clumsy header onto the flat, rolling lawns.

Not very expert, he realized as he hit down hard. More like a heavy box bouncing out the back of a speeding truck.

Except that when he stopped bouncing, he was still alive. Chewing dirt, as Sergeant P. Macdonald once instructed new men in the field.

And Johnson was still screaming like an agonized madman. *"Stay down, Macdonald! Stay there! . . . Stay there, Peter!"*

Up near the clubhouse, Peter spotted the shadow of a man with a rifle. The blond man? One of Hill's people? Too dark to be sure.

His heart started to pound so hard, he couldn't catch his breath. His mind filled with choking rage. He wanted the bastard so badly! It was fucked up, pathetic as hell—it was against everything he'd been trying to make of himself since Vietnam. But he wanted the man all the same. He wanted him so badly it ached. Infinite pain . . . why didn't you shoot me, you prick?

Suddenly automatic rifle fire came out of a grove of trees to his right. Rifles winked in the night. Licks of orange flame.

As he looked on, bullets mercilessly ripped and pounded the clubhouse. Expensive windows crumbled out of the dining room. Lights broke all over. A drainpipe was blown off a wall like papier-mâché.

Peter carefully aimed the Walther at the shadowy man. He squeezed off a single wild shot. A long, impossible shot that came surprisingly close. Then the shadow with the rifle was gone. All the shooting stopped, and it started to rain.

"Fuck you!" Peter stood up in the rain and shouted.

"Fuck you!

"Fuck you, you lousy son of a bitch!"

Sheets of rain came in cool, streaming torrents—making it nearly impossible to see. Like having a gunfight in a waterfall. Total confusion.

Somehow or other, he was thinking, Clive Lawson—late guttersnipe out of Billingsgate, late of the British Commandos, late of the unannounced Third World wars—had gotten himself into a nasty little booby trap. . . .

There'd been no word around that Damian and Carrie Rose were doubled dealers. Quite the opposite, in fact. . . . Christ! Why hadn't he stayed in Miami! Lived to fight another day?

The mercenary lay sideways like a hurt fish in a stonework gutter. He groped around for a flesh wound and found his left side to be numb. Then it burned as if he'd set a gasoline torch to himself.

Lawson turned his left arm to his face. Looked at the glowing silver dials on his watch: 9:12. Too bloody bad. His escape had been arranged for nine. Right after he'd gunned down Campbell. The Roses were supposed to get him out of there. Supposed to.

He started to crawl on his belly inside the littered gutter. He made little fish-fin strokes with his hands.

Then, at the end of the gutter, Clive Lawson got up and started to run.

Damian was God—slowly counting off the final few seconds of confusion.

He studied the teeming grounds through a light intensifier mounted on the stock of his sniper's rifle. The sighting device let him see in the dark. It threw whatever was in the rifle scope into a clear circle of eerie, Christmas-green light.

Watching the human vignettes in the strange green light, he slid his index finger gently down onto the rifle trigger. His finger took in the slack of the trigger. . . .

Peter's face was so wet, it was a bitch just to stop his eyes from blinking. Rainwater was rushing off his forehead. Rolling off his nose. He was actually choking on the rain. Getting frightened now because he couldn't see.

There was no sound around him except for the downpour and his own heavy breathing. His mind was racing at a madhouse pace. Throwing out Technicolor combat images, firefight scenes, disconnected phrases.

Up ahead he could see the outline of overturned furniture on a dining veranda. Wrought-iron tables and chairs. Broken plants and flower pots.

He took one more step forward. . . .

Then Peter saw the shape of another man across the open-air patio.

The man was crouching in front of baby palm trees. So far, he didn't realize that someone was on the terrace with him.

Peter used the cover of the loud rain to circle around closer. Inch by inch he got ten feet closer. Fifteen feet . . . another ten feet and he thought he would have a decent pistol shot.

He conned his mind into thinking that he couldn't miss, not even in the rain. He would squeeze off at least two quick shots, he knew. Then as many more shots as he could get in. He hoped the man would never get to use his Uzi.

Then the tall man actually began to move closer to him. He was moving sideways in a crouch, and he still had his back to Peter. He was moving like a professional army man.

Peter wiped the back of his hand across his eyes. The rainwater made them sting like hell. Now he could see that the man's hair was blond.

There is no way I can miss hitting this man, he reminded himself. Zen marksmanship. It's like standing twenty paces away from one of those big overturned dining tables. Taking your damn good time for a shot. Seeing not whether you hit it, but how close you can come to the little hole in the center for the table's umbrella.

How close can I come to the axis of the tall blond man's spine?

Kneeling on one knee, arms out stiff, perfectly

straight, two hands on the Walther, Peter carefully got the blond man in his sight. He brought an image of the first machete murder into his mind. Then Jane—Jane on the beach at Horseshoe Bay, her shrunken body in the coffin in the cathedral.

He looked straight down the black barrel into the man's back. Then Peter finally spoke to the tall blond man.

"Hey!" he said. "Do you remember me, mister? Hey, shithead!"

Inside the Tryall clubhouse, a nervous police constable lit a stick match.

As he struck match after match, the policeman tried desperately to figure out a row of master switches inside a steel gray cabinet. He considered the switches until his last match burned down, then decided to give number one a try. He flicked the black switch and the lights in the small room he was in came on bright and scary. Then the constable could see two distinct rows in the control box: number one through six, and seven through twelve.

His shaking hand moved quickly down the first row.

As the man on the dining veranda pivoted around to face Peter, every light in this magnificently frightening world seemed to come on all at once. Nightlights blinked on down the first fairway. A tape system on the veranda started to play soft dinner music.

Then loud thunder seemed to originate on the back patio of the Tryall clubhouse. Sparks of gunfire lit up all over the lawns.

Damian Rose was firing his M-21. Harold Hill was shooting an expensive Italian-made rifle. The entire force surrounding the Tryall clubhouse was blasting away at the suddenly bright, white building.

Peter's first shot hit the blond man—a dark hole opened on his forehead; then Peter was hit so hard, he couldn't believe it. He felt as if he'd been blindsided by a three-thousand-pound automobile. Hit deliberately. So fucking sad. So sad. . . .

Windows were breaking everywhere. The wrought-iron furniture was ringing out *pings* and *pangs*. Wood thudded hard as it caught errant rifle shots.

A singularly loud crack echoed, and a speck of the dead Englishman's head flew off.

The fallen Englishman was hit again on the side of his face.

A third rifle shot entered the back of his head as he lay facedown on the flagstone patio.

Then it was all blinding light and rain. Clean rain that appeared slightly blue in the white light. It was all soothing, steady rain noise with no gunshots at all.

Men streamed across the flat, muddy lawns. . . . Gray suits soaked to darker colors. Short pants and pillbox hats. Submachine guns and pistols and dark rifles swinging loose on leather straps.

The rain was shining like expensive jewelry in all the trees. There was an eerie quiet now.

Harold Hill was walking straight ahead, looking ridiculous, as if he were lost in the rain. His Top-Siders slapped down on the patio near Peter Macdonald's head, then he turned away.

Peter felt himself getting sick, and he fought the nauseated feeling with everything he had left.

A circle of curious faces began to form over him—like doctors around an operating table, like people staring at a heart attack victim on a New York City street. . . . Black soldiers and FBI and CIA men. All smiling as if they were his old best friends. Congratulating him as if he'd scored the winning touchdown.

The black police chief was bending over him, trying to show him where he'd been hit. The stomach? The rib cage? Goddamn nice bastard, Peter thought. "I'm okay." He grinned at the black man.

And in the middle of all the confusion—the blinding lights, rain, police sirens, an ambulance driving up on the lawns—a bearded white man in a suit was dragging a corpse by its hair. Some bearded CIA prick.

A creepy black policeman was snapping flashbulb

photos. Spread-eagle shots of the body that was being dragged. Shots of Peter being cradled in Meral Johnson's arms.

An American man was working with a buzzing electric camera that took pictures in the dark.

Suddenly they brought the body to Peter, and everybody was trying to talk to him all at one time. Peter sat up and waved them away. He stared down at bloodshot eyes turned up as far as they would go in their sockets. Eyes caught in terrible shock and surprise.

No wonder, though, Peter thought. The right side of the head looked as if it had been bitten into. There was no nose to speak of; what was left of the mouth was frozen in a smirky death cry.

Peter flashed back to Turtle Bay—the tall, haughty man. Fifteen seconds. . . .

He concentrated on the blown-up face. Wet blond hair slicked down flat by the rain. Long, athletic body. He felt very tired now, mind fighting against big strong waves of ugly shit. . . . Dr. Johnson was saying something to him, but all he felt like doing was shouting at the dead man.

"He's the one," he finally whispered to the black police chief. "He's the one, goddamn him to hell."

Which was about the time Peter finally heard what Meral Johnson was saying to him.

* * *

Running in a low infantry crouch, Damian moved forward, his trooper boots squishing across a slippery wooden ramp at the Tryall Club's yacht basin. He climbed movable stairs down onto the floating dock, stepped into the lurching Bertram Sportsman, and began to smile in spite of himself.

Then he began to laugh. A chilly, unnatural laugh.

He could barely distinguish voices in the distant, babbling commotion coming from up around the main clubhouse. He saw the thousand-watt floodlights flashing through swaying palm and banana trees up and down the first fairway.

Then the bouncing red lights of two ambulances turned a corner of the clubhouse building. Siren screams cut through the rain and wind like sharp knives.

Finally, after more than a year, after the most insanely exhausting ordeal he'd ever put himself through, it was over and done with.

Up on the Tryall Club's veranda, the ex–Green Beret, all-American boy, unimpeachable witness, had identified Clive Lawson as the tall blond man from Turtle Bay. . . . The English killer's hair, his hairstyle, height, facial features, were nearly identical with the man Macdonald had seen April 25. At a quick glance, Rose and Lawson were lookalikes—and a glance was all Peter had ever had. Fifteen seconds on a bicycle.

Moreover, the way Lawson's face wound up, it was academic anyway.

The great Damian Rose was officially dead. Killed on his most audacious tympanic contract. The psychological logic of the ploy was classic. Hubris struck again. Precisely the end they all would have predicted from him. Like Evel Knievel dying on a motorcycle.

Now, if Carrie succeeded in Washington, they were home free. No one would come looking for the Roses for quite some time. Maybe not ever.

Another smile drifted over Damian's thin, pretty lips. The pure satisfaction of playing the game well. The absolute, spine-tingling beauty of it. Like having built one's own cathedral in this slapdash age.

Moving quickly but quietly, Rose started the blowers, then untied the Dacron stern line that held the Sportsman to San Dominica. The twenty-five-foot speedboat was shaking like mere flotsam in the unsteady sea; the rain continued to teem.

As he unlooped a final knot in the bowline, a man appeared in the hatchway, coming from the sleeping cabin below. The man was tall and thin, dressed in a gray slicker with a hood. He threw back the hood, and his silver-gray hair completed the perfect yacht clubber image.

"Hello, there," the dark figure said. "My name is Harold Hill. I thought we should meet."

The director of Great Western Air Transport hoisted himself into the stormy cockpit. Harry the Hack. Dependable Harry.

"Actually, you do nice work." He continued to speak as he climbed up top. "Stay put, now. Don't get up on my account. Don't move a fucking muscle."

Pointing a dark Walther at the younger man's heart, Hill rested his bottom on the back of a swivel chair.

"Hair dyed a nice shade of black." He showed his teeth in an appreciative smile. "Cut to look like some goober from Lithuania. That's nice. What did you plan to do from here?"

Damian tried to keep himself calm. Icy. Think straight lines. Think nothing but straight lines. As he spoke, his mind raced back and forth through his alternatives, through all the possibilities for this situation.

"I was going to take a commercial flight off the island." He spoke softly. At the same time, he was thinking that something about Harold Hill was bothering him; he couldn't put his finger on it exactly. "Now that I'm officially dead, you know."

"Macdonald isn't, you know," Harold Hill said. "I'm curious—why didn't you kill Macdonald, too? The famous last shoot-out scenario?"

"I thought a live witness would be more convincing in the long run. Don't you think? . . . Macdonald was part of all this from the start, you know."

Hill seemed a bit confused. "Macdonald was working for you? . . ."

Don't laugh at him, Damian thought. Don't laugh in his face. . . .

"No. No . . . but right from the beginning we knew we'd need a witness to identify Lawson. To make our escape work right . . . we knew that Peter Macdonald rode around Turtle Bay every afternoon. So we planned a murder right there. *C'est ça.* Macdonald saw me because he was meant to see me. We even went to great lengths to strengthen his credibility afterward. . . . Tell me something. Did Carrie do this?"

Harold Hill shook his head from side to side. "*I* ask the questions." The CIA director smiled and motioned for the younger man to get up. Slowly.

As he stood, Hill knocked Rose back down with a gun-butt blow to the cheek. A vicious hit.

"Best I can do right now," Hill said through clenched teeth. "For Carole. My wife. . . . Get up now. I won't hit you anymore. I have lots of questions before I kill you, Rose. I have an interesting idea for that, too."

His mouth all bloody, Damian got up again. He held his hands high, in plain sight. Like a magician about to do a trick.

At Hill's direction, Rose took hold of the ladder going up to the dock. "On our way across the lawn"—he spoke in calm, measured tones—"I want you to listen carefully to what I have to offer you. We can renew our partnership."

As the tall dark-haired man put both hands on the metal ladder, the right side of his head exploded.

His face crashed forward against the aluminum slats. His chin bounced down two rungs, then he fell over backward into the boat.

Harold Hill looked up to find the black police chief standing on the wooden ramp. Beside him was Macdonald, slightly bent over, holding a Walther pointed down at the boat.

"We followed you," Meral Johnson said simply. Peter Macdonald said nothing.

As Hill started to climb past the dead or dying man, he saw the sugar-cane machete lying across a leather seat. The most obscene murder weapon. The cleaver they'd used on Carole in Virginia.

In one unbelievable stroke, he brought it down powerfully across Rose's face. The hacking blow made a noise like a butcher's cleaver. Damian snorted like a horse.

The field machete came down again. A clumsy guillotine.

Finally Hill kicked the head and it sloshed up against a sideboard. Floated in a dark pool of rainwater.

Then Harold Hill climbed up the movable ladder. He said nothing to the black policeman; nothing to Peter.

"What partnership was that?" Peter said. Then he let it go . . . let the sentence evaporate in the night air. It didn't matter. Of course the CIA was in on it. . . .

For a long moment they all stood on the wet ramp. The black man and the young white man close together. None of them speaking. . . . Then Hill untied the last restraining rope. It doesn't end, the CIA man was thinking. Now these two have to be taken care of. . . .

As the Sportsman slowly drifted away, Meral Johnson fired several shots into the boat's bottom and sides. "Let the fish have him," the black man said.

At first Harold Hill's hands were trembling. Then, very slowly, the director began to feel rather good. In a way, he supposed, he was the hero of it all: the man who saved Central Intelligence.

Or maybe it was Carrie Rose who was the heroine.

After all, it was Carrie who'd phoned the embassy to tell him how to get Damian; who'd revealed the last details of the monster plot. . . . He should have told Rose that, Hill thought too late. He should have told Damian that, in the end, Carrie had turned on him and set him up. How very fucking pathetic.

The woman he'd slept with for nine years—loved, presumably. His protégée, among other things. . . . Well, she was going to get hers, too . . . a perfect ending.

For a long time the three men stood in the rain, watching the speedboat drift away. Listening to the gulps of the bobbing, sinking boat.

"Peter asked you a question before," Meral Johnson said. "What kind of partnership did you have with him?"

Suddenly Peter raised the Walther again. Sideways. Almost without looking, it seemed, the force of the single pistol shot knocked Hill ten feet out onto the water.

"Let the fish have both of them," Peter said.

He and the short, fat policeman walked slowly back to the clubhouse.

May 12, 1979, Saturday
Raid
St. James

May 12, 1979; Washington, D.C.

Saturday Morning.

At quarter past six on the morning of the twelfth, two heavyweights from Langley—twenty-seven-year-old Alex Fletcher and Deputy John Devereaux—stepped out of a white Pontiac Le Mans, then ran across the dewy back lawns of the sedate, prohibitively expensive St. James Hotel.

Inside the fancy hotel, some of America's richer and more noted personages were fast asleep on the already pretty, blue-skied spring morning. Outside on the manicured back lawns, blackbirds were just beginning to make their little peeps and tuwitts. One hale fellow disappeared over the garden fence as if he were going to fetch the morning's *Post*.

Alex Fletcher was wearing a film director's bush

jacket and brushed corduroys, with a Smith & Wesson .38 strapped across a cotton workshirt.

Devereaux, fifty-six years old, wore a dark suit with an open-necked white shirt. A cigarette hung from his lower lip like a piece of white tape.

The two men sneaked inside the gray metal door rarely used by anyone but St. James's maintenance men. Behind the door they found a security guard asleep with a white Siamese cat on his belly. The man had passed out on a folding beach chair and was snoring like broken-down machinery.

"Good morning." Devereaux grinned. "Monsieur Le Chat."

"Some fucking joint," Fletcher whispered. "No wonder the D.C. police have such a big, throbbing dick of a job."

The two men proceeded up battleship gray back stairs, uncarpeted and unexpectedly dreary. A smelly cat litter box sat on one stairwell. They came out into an elegant hallway marked with a big pink five on powder blue walls.

Fletcher whistled under his breath. "Now this is more like it."

The young agent tapped a real crystal chandelier with his fingernail. "Class, Devereaux, class."

"I'll buy it for you and your girlfriend," John Devereaux growled. "Right after we finish our business here. Present arms!"

The two men stopped in front of room 502. Big

gold numbers on the softest powder blue. Tasteful molding. Escarping.

Alex Fletcher took a deep breath, whispered a cynical ejaculation, then slowly slid a hotel passkey into the lock.

The deputy brought a .44 Magnum out from under his sports jacket, a loud, dangerous cannon young Fletcher disapproved of entirely. "Nuclear warfare," he'd nicknamed the long black pistol.

He gave Devereaux a funny little smile. "Try not to blow me up by mistake. Just a passing thought. Ready?"

"For Harold Hill and Carole."

"Mmm."

The elaborate door swung over thick mauve carpeting. The two agents looked in on a light-haired woman sitting up in a rumpled double bed. A big room full of morning sun.

"Who are you?" the long-haired woman said. She reached toward her night table.

"No!" Fletcher screamed—the absolute top volume of his voice.

Then Devereaux's .44 detonated in the doorway.

The astonished woman literally flew against the red velvet wall, the brass headrails of her bed. She gave out one small groan, and her green eyes rolled back. Then Betsy Port-Smithe slowly slid down to the floor.

Young Fletcher frowned and shook his head.

"No questions. No answers." The ambitious agent kicked over an end table. "Shit. Shit, Devereaux."

Devereaux shrugged. He sniffed the air. A funny combination of Joy perfume and smoky cordite.

The deputy threw open a window on Rock Creek Park, then stood there going through the woman's suede pocketbook. Inside he found letters from a man named Damian; he found cards and papers that identified Carrie Rose. . . . Inside the night table drawer he found a small .38 revolver.

"Better call them." Devereaux smiled. "Tell them they can stop worrying about this shitty bastard Mrs. Rose. No scandals in the White House for today."

Like Harold Hill, fifty-six-year-old John Devereaux was thinking that he was a hero, too. They'd told him not to bring her back alive.

The Season of the Machete was finally over.

THE
EPILOGUE

The Summer Season

CHAPTER TWENTY-NINE

I am Superwoman . . . SuperRat . . .
Superscuz . . . Damian trained me so that
I was capable of anything—then he let me
do nothing. Stagnate. He would have
never even let me sell my diary. When his
own obsessions became impossible—a
liability to both of us—I had to kill him.
No choice in the matter. <u>Had to</u> . . . now
I'm all alone at the top of the heap. The
first Public Enemy on the loose in
decades. . . . My prices start at $1,000,000,
and I'm worth it. I'm like a Paris original, a
one-of-a-kind operation. Hiring me is like
being able to hire Manson, Speck,
Himmler, Bormann . . . I'll do anything
you can think of, and I'll think of things
you wouldn't. The Season of the Machete
was a preamble—as primitive as its
name. It was just a beginning. The Tool
Age of violence and disruption . . . now

comes the interesting part. We're just
entering the Machine Age, I believe.

The Rose Diary

June 13, 1979; Coastown, San Dominica

Feeling like a national hero, Prime Minister Joseph Walthey paraded through large, enthusiastic crowds in Coastown's Horseshoe Beach District.

Paid admirers—civil servants, especially—circled him like birds. They patted his cream suede suit jacket, reached out for his curly, slicked-down hair, reached to touch his round, black Santa Claus face.

Thirty-five-millimeter news footage was shot for special release to San Dominica's thirteen movie theaters. Hundreds of publicity photographs were taken for the world's newspapers.

At a high, colorful dais built over the boardwalk, over the shimmering Caribbean, Walthey announced that an era of new prosperity was dawning for San Dominica. The smiling, affable prime minister didn't elaborate, however.

July 14, 1979; Coastown, San Dominica

In a special session of the San Dominican Assembly, Prime Minister Joseph Walthey was named president for life on the island. He made a long speech about nationalism, the economy, and tourism on San Dominica: he lied at length.

October 1, 1979; Turtle Bay, San Dominica

The first casino to open on San Dominica was in the Playboy Club—not five miles from the Plantation Inn.

The grand opening was marred by minor student demonstrations. Black boys and girls waved a psychedelic poster of Dassie Dred that was making the rounds at the University of the West Indies and other schools throughout Central and South America. They played loud reggae and soul music, and some cars and walls at the Playboy were spray-painted DRED! The students waved signs that read JOE IS THE BLACK HITLER.

March 3, 1980; Zurich, Switzerland

Nearly ten months after Damian's death, on the afternoon of March 3, 1980; 4.5 million Swiss francs were deposited in the numbered account of Mrs. Susan Chaplin in the Schweizer Kreditverein in Zurich. The money represented nearly $2 million from the diary sale.

Curiously, three days after her withdrawal of $600,000 (American) in May of 1979 (a Damian-style safeguard—what if he had eluded Hill at the Tryall Club?), the woman had redeposited her money in a new account.

Filling out the necessary tax forms for the 1980 deposit, S. O. Rogin found himself thinking once again of Mrs. Chaplin in terms of the actress Faye Dunaway. So many actors and actresses, the red-faced munchkin thought. All the world a stage for these Americans.

May 9, 1981; Paris

Peter Macdonald had begun to wear the same Harris Tweed jacket every day, the same green crew-neck sweater. His brown hair fell down over his white shirt collars now, and he had a thick, bushy mustache.

Each morning from ten to eleven he sat in the same St.-Germain-des-Prés cafes—Flore, Deux Magots, occasionally Brasserie Lipp. He always drank cafe au lait, read the *International Herald-Tribune*, watched the pretty women like any other

American in Paris. Occasionally he even read the obscene, arrogant diary.

Beside Peter at the cafe table, Meral Johnson sat and ate half a dozen biscuits with his tea. Antagonist of the Joseph Walthey regime and the Central Intelligence Agency, currently on permanent leave from the San Dominican police force, Johnson exerted a steadying influence on Peter here in France. He was his traveling partner and occasionally his Dutch uncle as well.

According to their latest plan, they would spend at least the next six months in Europe. In and around Paris . . . down on the Riviera in Nice . . . in Zurich around the Stampfenbachstrasse. Whatever it took.

Paris was nice in May, Peter thought as he sipped his coffee this particular morning. It wasn't the sunny Caribbean, there was no Jane to share it with him, but Paris was quite acceptable, to his way of thinking.

At ten-thirty that morning, a hip little Frenchman carrying a thick leather valise approached. He sat with them at their cafe table.

"You are the men who look for Carrie Rose?" the Frenchman asked.